LETTARS FROM AN IMBECILE

AARON-BAKPORHE UFUOMA

Published by
Omojojolo Books
An Imprint of Emotion Press
Jakan Street, Agbowo Express, Agbowo, Ibadan
info@omojojolo.com, www.omojojolo.com
info@ufuomabakporhe.com, www.ufuomabakporhe.com.

First published in 2014

ISBN: 978-978-943-377-3

Nextlink Prints

Dedication

To Dad, for inspiring me to write and for
believing in me. I miss you.

ACKNOWLEDGEMENT

My family, dad, Late chief(Sir)Aaron Bakporhe for being my inspiration and literary guide, to mum, Lady(Mrs) Mary Bakporhe, to my aunty Gina, for being a huge support. To my siblings, Akpevwe, Ogaga, Kohwo for every bit of contribution that they made during the whole process concerning the production of the book. To Yemi Ijomone, for her support.

To my friends from school, Christabel Eguriase, my friend and little proof reader of every piece I wrote, Claret Atsiangbe, Ize-Iyamu Rhoda and Gift Esimikhe for their words of encouragement and being the bestfriends I could ever ask for, Etefe Voke, Alabi Emilia, Oke Onobraekpeyan, Idris Adebayo, Joe Chikezie, Christabel Ahweyevu, Aziegbe Rita, Obarho Oferiofe and a whole set of friends who believed in my writing and supported me all the way from the beginning till now.

To Folarin Olaniyi, the wonder and wonderful editor, for your words of encouragement and advice all the way and a splendid job. To Lola Sanusi, for loving the book so much. To God Almighty, for making this a success. Amen. Thank you all.

1

Dear lettar,

Hawa you? Do you know my name? You bon't know my name. My name is Atarhe Okeoghene Onanefe. Is it long? Everything is not my name oooo. The first two are my names whirl the last one is my Papa's name. My Papa boesn't like me like he likes my sistar, Omotejohwo. We call her Johwo. Papa saib that I yam an imbecill, a bunbie and so he prefer to have my Mama dorn a dady doy than dorn me. Papa hate me. Lettar, do you know that everybay I use to cry decause I yam afraib of him. I always fear when he comes to home. I use to go and hibe unber my deb that have tear every where. The foam have tear that all those yellow colour will now de showing when there is no debspread dut me and my sistar still sleep on it like that sha. I want to tell you something lettar, dut bon't tell another person oooo. Dib you hear? I bon't know if my sistar likes me decause I used to fear to tell her things. She is smaller than me decause I yam senior to her dut I know she is senior to me in the drain. She is very inteligent. I bon't use to talk to my neighbours chilbren too. Lettar, you know, I think I used to fear too much. I yam always afraib. Lettar, will you de my destfrienb. I bon't have any frienbs dut if you agree to de my

5

destfriend, I will always de happy. So, will you de my destfrienb? If you agree to de my frienb, I will not de fearing again like defore. I will always be happy anb cry anb fear will not come again. Lettar, what language are you? I bon't know French I would have used it to talk to you. So, we will manage English ehn.' Is my hanbwriting fine? You bon't want to tell me. Mayde it is not fine. Bon't worry, I know you will say it when next we talk. Will you please smile for me? Ok, mayde you have not make frienbs with me yet or you have not hear the question anb finish. I will talk to you letar. Bye bye. Oya, go and rest.

Your frienb,
Atarhe

That was the first letter. I usually kept the letters under my bed, inside a small blue bucket. It was the bucket that Mama bought for both of us to bathe with. I and Johwo had bathed with it for two days, the bucket fell from my hands as I was fetching water from the tap at the backyard. It fell hard on the stone Mama had placed to support buckets, and to keep them from touching the sand on the ground and getting dirty. Immediately the bucket landed on the stone, it gave a loud noise and it busted. I was very scared to tell Mama but when I did, she did not punish me as Papa would have done. I knew Mama was not going to beat me. She had never done that, but I was naturally a very scared person. She said she was going to throw the bucket away. But the bucket was blue. I loved blue. I asked Mama to let me have the bucket. Mama let me have it. I did not know if I would have need of it as at that time. I only wanted it for keeps

6

then because of the colour. Mama always granted my requests. I could hardly think of any one that she had not granted. So that was where I kept my letters. They were safe there.

Papa was a catechist at St. Andrews Catholic Church, Ughelli. We worshipped there. He was born into the catholic family and so he raised us his children in the Catholic faith. He always wore either a dark blue dress like the parish priest's cassock and at other times, it was green of that same material and design. Mama told us that Papa had studied for a long time in a school somewhere in Ekpoma before he became a full catechist. I wondered how the school would be. Men wearing garments and learning in class rooms like little children. It would be funny. When I was much younger, I used to tell people that Papa was a priest, a *fada*. It was not until I was old enough that I grew to understand that he was a catechist and not a priest. Priests did not have wives or children. They were kept aside for God - they and the Reverend Sisters.

Every Sunday, we drove to church in Papa's cargo motorcycle. I would stay at the back seat with Mama while Johwo would sit on the fuel tank in front. The tank was red in colour. Bloodshot red. The Cycle had been Papa's since I could remember. The seats have worn out that they were crying out to be coated with new leather. Papa drove it in the same state not minding the look. He did not have enough money for the family let alone for motorcycle repairs. As long as he could drive it, it was okay for him. His meagre allowance from the church was not enough to carry out all our needs even when added to his income from farm work. Johwo always enjoyed the ride on the tank. A lot of children enjoyed it also. I used to enjoy it when I was much younger. Sitting on the tank, you would always get a clear view and soft breeze blowing into your face. I only did not enjoy tank riding when there is a heavy wind coming especially during the rains. It was also very uncomfortable at such times.

Mass was always at 8 o'clock in the morning but we made sure to get there by 7 o'clock every Sunday. This was because Papa led the opening prayers every Sunday and weekday Masses. If there was a feast or an occasion, it would be announced that Mass was shifted to another time. We usually had one mass on Sundays. After the prayers, Papa would say the Mass intentions. Then, Mass would begin and after the liturgy, Father Sixtus would preach for two hours. Though I enjoyed his teaching that did not keep me from sleeping throughout most of the homily. Mama would give me a stroke. I would wake up, say I was not sleeping and try to keep my eyes open but in the next two minutes, I would find them shut again. Then, Mama would let me sleep undisturbed for the remaining part of the homily. She would then wake me up when it was time for the Apostle's creed which was the proclamation of the Catholic faith. We never sat with Papa. He was always in the first pew on the left row. The creed was usually said before the Prayers of the Faithful except on week day Masses. It would be at that time that I would stand and mumble the little parts of the creed that I knew. I had failed catechism class twice, and I was unable to receive the Sacrament of the Holy Eucharist. Papa had called me dumb head at those times and stopped me from taking more classes as he believed that I would disgrace him again. Johwo was going to receive the sacrament next Christmas. I was not jealous of her. I was happy for her because I knew that one day I would also receive the blessed sacrament.

When Mass was over, we would stay with Mama and wait for Papa to round up his discussion with people so that we could all go to greet Father Sixtus. Father Sixtus was a young priest. He had been in the priesthood for only seven years. He was transferred to our parish two years ago. Father Sixtus always called me by my second name, Oke. It meant gift. He told my parents that I was a gift to the family. He always asked how I was in a specific manner every Sunday.

'Oke, how are you?'

I always had the answer memorised in my brain and I opened my mouth to let it out. It was a Sunday routine for us. Father Sixtus and I.

'I yam doing fine, fada.' I would say. He would ask Johwo the same question and she would answer. Unlike me, she had series of ways to answer the question. In different ways she would answer him. 'I am fine, Father,' 'Father, I am very fine,' 'Father, I am great' 'Father, you know that I am always fine.' She had tons of her replies. I had just one and I stuck to it. Maybe I feared that I would make a mistake if I changed it. Johwo is a very beautiful girl. Papa loved her a lot. She is intelligent and good-looking. She had this beautiful brown eyes that drew attention to her. Her nose is pointed almost as the edge of Bic pen. At times, I feared that she would injure her hands if she touched the tip of her nose. She has a beautifully formed lips that were not full in contrast with mine that were as full as newly baked bread. She has chubby cheeks unlike my sullen cheeks. She was light-skinned like Mama and when she was upset, those cheeks turned pink. I was absolutely the ugly duckling of the family, it was no wonder that Papa favoured her. As a catechist, it would be expected of Papa to treat us, his children, equally but I do not blame him. Not everyone could have accepted a child like me. It was not easy being Papa's child. My medical problem was a hindrance. I was mentally slow and Papa referred to me as an imbecile. He said that if not for the fact I did not drool, I would have been a complete imbecile. His words were always harsh and it was as if I had made myself that way. I always kept quiet and when I get home from school, I stayed in my room reading the papers or novels or story books that I could find. Reading was a major problem for me and so was spelling but I read all the same, mistaking one word for the other. I read them the best way I could not minding the meanings. I always found myself enjoying reading.

After Sunday mass, we went home to a meal of rice and stew which Mama had prepared in the morning before we went to church. The stew usually contained pieces of fried fish. Mama preferred fish to beef because it was usually cheaper. The head and tail was always reserved for Papa. I wondered if Mama gave Papa the head because he was the

10

head of the family. Maybe fathers were meant to eat the head of fish. Once I asked Mama if Papa would also eat the head of the cow if she had prepared the stew with beef. Mama laughed and said that we could not cook the head but pieces of the meat chopped off the head of the cow. I did not understand what she meant.

'Mama, are you saying that we all take part in eating the head of the *malu?* I imagined us all tearing from the head of the cow placed in a big bowl.

'No, Atarhe. We don't eat the head but the meat in the head of the cow,' she explained.

'But Mama, is it not the same thing you are saying?'

Mama laughed. 'Okay, it is the same thing, my child'

Mama will never spend enough time arguing with me. She did not want to fill my sick head with things that she thought would confuse me. I was a ten year old girl in primary two. When my mental retardation was discovered, Mama and Papa had sent me to school at the age of five. Two years after the normal age of schooling. I started kindergarten in Local Government Nursery School, Ughelli. I was slow and I had to repeat my KG 1 and then I scaled through the rest of Kindergarten. Mama enrolled me in Community Primary school, Ughelli. I was also having problems here but Mama had me pushed till I got to primary two.

This Sunday, we came back from church and ate our food in silence. I broke the silence when I spoke of my home work.

'Mama, they gave us homework in school to do and I don't understand it. I have tried my best to do it but it is hard to do.' I never told Papa of my homework. It was always Mama.

'What is the assignment about?' Papa asked. I did not respond. I was scared anytime Papa interfered in my school issues.

'Atarhe! Did you hear?'

'Yes, Papa.' I answered with my head bowed low; staring at my laps like Papa's face was drawn there. He looked sternly at me.

'Atarhe, answer your father. What is it about?' Mama said.

I gave no response.

'You don't want to answer, ehn? Ok, go and bring it and let me see,' Papa said.

I stood up slowly. My legs felt heavy to move. I was literally shaking. I did not want Papa to start abusing me for not being able to do what he would see as an easy work. I went to my room, scrabbled through my bag and brought out my Mathematics note. I went back to the parlour which we also used as our dining table. We placed our food on the stools or on the coffee table to eat. I gave Papa my notebook. He opened to the last page where the homework was written. He laughed aloud like someone in an AY live comedy show. I looked at him in the same manner a lost puppy would look when it was hungry for food.

'Onimerire, see what your daughter cannot solve at her age?'

'Let me see, Papa Atarhe.' That was what Mama called him. She never called him by his name. Only the church people called him Catechist Joseph or Josefu as the old and local members of the church pronounced. Mama took the book and looked at it.

'Don't worry, Atarhe. We will do it together,' Mama assured.

'Your sister is a class ahead of you. Why did you not ask her?' Papa asked.

Johwo looked at me. I turned my face away. I did not want to meet her eyes which would say *You see?*

'Papa Atarhe, please leave her alone. I will teach her.' Mama then turned to me and said. 'My dear, don't worry. Finish your food, we would sit and do it'

'That's how you spoil the girl,' Papa chided.

Mama said nothing nor did I. We finished eating in silence and Mama taught me the calculations in the assignment. We were to solve with the long division method and I got to understand a little as Mama explained. I was glad Mama had time to teach me. Now, I had something to submit in school the next day.

The next day, Papa dropped Johwo and myself at school. He rode us to school every morning and we trekked back after school in the afternoon. There were a lot of other pupils who did the *Legerdes* Benz every day after school. That was what we called it. I was not sure if I liked any of the teachers because none seemed to like me. They treated me like a child with no future ambition. Some even called me NFA, an acronym for it. School was more hell than home for me. This morning we had to submit our Mathematics homework. I had submitted and got all five questions right. Mrs Okorodafe was surprised at my excellence and called me to do the corrections. I walked to the board and then it all went blank. All that Mama had taught me suddenly seemed to have disappeared from my memory. I took the white chalk from her hand and went to the board. The black board that the big boys in school used to darken every Friday with the black substance found in batteries. The question was to divide 125 by 5 using the long division process. I drew the division sign which I always drew as a small square first and then erased the first and cleaned the right side and the lower line. I wrote in the numbers in the correct form with the first number inside the division sign and the lower one on the top line. I could not do the calculations anymore. I knew the answer ended on the number five but I could not do calculations and could not remember the digits. I finally scribbled something down. I wrote 105 as my answer. I did not do any solving, I just wrote it. I had no idea why I wrote it down. I turned and said,

'Aunty, I have finish the work'

'Atarhe, no solving and you have an answer?'

I nodded my head. She turned to the class.

'Class, is she correct?'

'No!' the intelligent students topped the response. I could see Gift, Adaora and Benson shouting on top of their voices to be heard. They were the three best students in the class. Gift and I never looked at each other's side for once. She was almost a bully.

'You are wrong, Atarhe. So, tell me how you got all five questions and number one is even the simplest of them all, yet you cannot do the correction?'

'Mama and I did it yesterday' I answered.

'Your mother did your homework for you?' she asked, almost in a raging voice.

'No, Aunty,'

'Then?' The class was quiet. Everyone wanted to hear and see what would happen next. You could hear no voice. Only the whirr of the two fans was heard.

'She taught me but I have forgotten, Aunty,' I said. The words just came out like I was spitting out hot yam.

'Just as I expected. I do not know why your parents keep you here. How were you even admitted? Your parents should look for a special school for you or send you to learn a trade'. She said it with all its coldness. I felt cold run down my spine like ice cubes. I started sobbing silently. It was silent enough to be unheard but I was sobbing. I did not know whether to look at her, whether to say I was sorry or not.

'Atarhe, how old are you?'

This was not the first time Mrs Okorodafe or any other teacher would be asking me that question. *I yam ten years old.'* The words were on my lips. I opened my mouth but they just would not come out. The tears ran slowly down my cheeks. I only knew they were flowing when my tongue tasted salt. Then, they begin to rush faster like the tap at our backyard. The whole class started laughing the leaders were Gift and her friends, Beatrice and Susan. They were laughing so hard that Mrs Okorodafe asked everyone to keep quiet.

'Atarhe, go to your seat'

I moved slowly to my seat and kept my head on the desk and continued crying. I did not if it was loud or not. I did not want to know. I sat on the third seat of the middle role. I sat at the right edge while Chinyere, another girl, sat at the left with a boy in our middle. His name was Dami. His mother was Yoruba but his father, Urhobo. He said she hails from Ondo state. Hence, he was named so. He patted my back and asked me to stop crying.

'Atarhe, stop crying,' he said.

I heard what he said clearly but I did not raise my head, respond or stop crying. The tears just kept flowing endlessly like a river. I only raised my head when I heard Aunty call my name.

'Atarhe'

'Aunty'

'Sit upright'

'Yes, Aunty.'

I wiped the tears off my cheeks and eyes slowly. My eyes had grown swollen like freshly ripe *ebelebo* fruits. I sat down to listen. The class just seemed to pass through my face. I was very upset. I said nothing during class. 10 o'clock was break time. Cries of children, 'Breaking time! Breaking time!' was heard. Then, you'd find pupils running down to the field, going to buy snacks and food. I usually went to

Johwo's class to call her. We would sit to eat the food Mama had dished in our food flask. The days we were not given food to school, we bought food with money Papa or Mama would give us. I usually let Johwo hold the food flask and money because I was certain no one could bully her for it. We ate in silence. Today, after eating, I had closed the flask and was about going back to my class.

'Did someone make you angry or sad?' She asked me.

'Ehn?'

'Why were you crying? See your eyes are like the colour of an over-ripe cherry. What is it?'

I shook my head. That Nothing was wrong.

'Someone insulted you, abi?' she asked, sounding like it was a normal affair for me to get insulted.

I shook my head again.

'Who is it?'

'Nobody,' I said, 'Leave me alone'

I left her and rushed to my class. I sat on my seat and placed my head on the desk again. I started crying again. The tears just kept flowing. Immediately school closed, I called Johwo and we walked home. She stopped to buy the yoghurt they sold on bicycles for fifty, seventy and hundred naira. She bought yoghurt worth of fifty naira. She did not bother buying for me. Everyone who knew me knew how much I hated yoghurt. It always felt like raw egg and coconut milk in my mouth. I would even prefer to drink from Mama's breast milk even if it was dry than have yoghurt. We got home and took off our uniforms throwing it all over the place. Mama let Johwo wash her uniform but she never let me wash mine. She washed it herself. She said I had never washed them clean.

'How was school today?' Mama asked

'It was fine, Mama,' I answered. I had no intentions of telling her what transpired in class.

'Mama, the teacher in school shouted at Atarhe for not remembering the solution to the assignment today,' Johwo reported, like she was a news correspondent.

'Johwo, keep quiet. Atarhe, is it true?'

I nodded slowly and I felt the tears roll down my cheeks again. They came just like they did in class. It was like they were put on repeat to keep rolling and rolling down.

'My dear, come'. Mama stretched her hand out for me to hold. She sat on the kitchen stool and made me sit on her laps.

'Mama, I'm hungry o,' Johwo said

'Okay soak *garri* and take one piece of dried fish from on top of the *itaso*,' Mama said.

Johwo took the fish from our kitchen at the backyard and went to the parlour and sat down to eat.

'Atarhe, my dear, what happened?'

I narrated the whole story to Mama. Mama asked that I do not worry or cry but I should forget about it. She said that whatever the problem was, it would be solved by God.

'But Mama why am I like this?'

'My daughter, you are like this because you are special. You are my Oke. That was why I told your father to name you that. You are a blessed child, do not cry or worry anymore.' She wiped my tears with the edge of her wrapper that she loosed off.

'Do you want fish?'

I nodded. 'Ehn'

'Okay, go and take it from the *itaso*'

I smiled. My teeth showed under my grin. Those were the only beautiful things in me, my teeth. Mama said they were bright white. I poured *garri* into my favourite blue plastic plate pouring it slowly with my hand raised high to make it look like rain falling. I pulled off one tied wrap of granulated sugar in it. We always bought them when we needed sugar. They were five naira per wrap. Mama never bought a carton of sugar. I cannot remember seeing the blue packet of St. Louis sugar in our house except if it was the part of the offertory from church which Father sometimes share with us. We never had to use milk to drink *garri*. Mama said it was waste of milk and so we ate it without milk. After lunch, I went to my room. There were no assignments and there were no new story books to read. I went to write my letters.

Dear lettar,

Hawa you tobay? I came from school and saib I shoulb come anb talk to you. Dib you miss me? I know you bib This is the seconb bay that we are talking. Lettar, bo you know what happened in school tobay? shey, you know that yesterbay Mama tought me the Maths homework. I went to school and aunty in class saib that I shoulb bo the correction that we always do after homewrok. I went to the dlackdoard dut I

19

forgot everything. I wrote the wrong answer and the class shamed me. I started crying. Do you know that nodoby in that school that is an aunty or uncle like me.' They have all been so unkinb to me and they make me cry everybay. Lettar, I want you to keep this as only us that know. I want them to dring a new ~~tich~~ teachar that will like me anb teach me anb make me dettar. You will like that, abi? Last time, you bib not tell me if my hanbwriting is good or not. I know it is not fine. The teachars call it fowl scratch. I bon't know why decause I bon't know how fowls scratch their doby but even if they scratch, I wonder how it lookeb, maybe it was really like the way I write. I yam hearing my sistar coming. She will ask what I yam boing. I will talk to you letar. Take care.

Your frienb,
Atarhe

I folded the paper immediately, drew the blue bucket located under my bed and threw the folded paper into it. I sat on the bed, staring at the ceiling. My eyes were set on it, as if the new teacher I wanted was sitting there and smiling at me. The image cleared out of my head when Johwo came in.

'What are you doing, Atarhe?' She called me by my name. She never called me sister like most other younger children did to their older ones. I wondered if I would have said sister to an elder sister, if I had one.

'Nothing, Johwo. I want to sleep. I am just tired'

'It would be because of all your crying. Don't cry again, you hear?' she said.

20

'I have heard you.' I did not know what more to say to Johwo.

'I am going to the parlour. They have brought the light. DRTV will be showing Tom & Jerry.' She ran out of the room straight to the parlour.

I lay on my bed and shut my eyes. I shut them from the walls of my room, I shut them from the world, I shut them from the bitterness I felt. I shut them from the fear that crept into my mind. I shut them from the pains I felt, from the insecurity that grew and I shut them from myself. I wanted a new fate, I wanted my voice to be heard, I wanted to be given a new name, I wanted to scream at the loudest but I could not find that voice. It shrunk within me. I let my subconscious take over and slept off. I had a dream. It was beautiful. I wished I would dream like that every other day.

2

Dear lettar

It is the thirb bay we have together. I bo not have much time decause I yam going for Mass now. Will talk after school.

Your frienb,
Atarhe

The letter was short that morning. It was just three sentences. It was a Tuesday. Every Tuesday morning, we went to the church for Mass. Papa dropped us at school afterwards. Mama would then go to her small kiosk where she sold biscuits, sweets and pure water. She comes home in the afternoon after we had arrived from school and serves our lunch, and then she can go back and trade. It is a stone's throw from our house and at times, we would go to the kiosk and sit with Mama watching as customers buy various items. Johwo enjoyed selling. I enjoyed the opportunity of getting sweets and other items from Mama. I always chose *Milkos* any time she asked me what I wanted. Maybe I liked it because the wrap had a spring of milk pouring over the candy. I loved milk. Cowbell Milk. I told Mama that *Milkos* had cowbell milk in it.

We got to school just as assembly was about to begin. The school children with their bags flung on their shoulders and backs stood on the queues. The school was filled with different types of pupils. Some of whom their uniforms were patched from tearing or were still torn in different places which was called post office. We said the holes were big enough to send letters. A post office was for sending and receiving letters. That was what we were taught. Papa sent letters to a priest in Rome every month and he received letters in return. He had said that it was through the post office that he sent and received them. I wished there was a post office to send my letters to myself. Assembly soon started and we listened to the announcements. After the announcement, we sang the National Anthem. Pupils ruined the National Anthem. I also did not know it very well. I joined the other pupils to sing along. *'Arise o compatriots, Nigeria call obey to serve our fathersland with love and strength and faith.......'* We sang it with all confidence, without noticing mistakes such as 'Fathersland' instead of 'Fatherland' and 'Nigeria' instead of 'Nigeria's' and a whole lot of others. We sang it that way every day and we got no corrections from the teachers. At the end of the assembly, primary two pupils were asked to raise the marching song. We started the song, although not in unison. *'O my home, my home/ when shall I see my home/ when shall I see my native land/ I will never forget my home.'* At the end of the song a loud and thunderous

23

'*Omyome, myome*' was heard. We sang and marched in long undisrupted lines to the classrooms. We feared the long cane of Mrs Rachel, the head teacher. Only the primary five students were courageous enough to fall out of their line.

Gift's friend, Beatrice walked up to me in class before the class teacher came in. Her aim was to make trouble like they always did.

'How are you?' she asked. It was more in a sarcastic tune than friendly. I did not give her a response. I was reading the back cover of my notebook which had the multiplication table. We always recited it every morning. I did not want another episode of embarrassment that morning. Beatrice was about seven years of age. She had a mouth with that words cut through someone's emotions like a razor. She and her friends picked on me a lot but I did not bother.

'Did you hear, ehn?'

'What na?' I asked.

'All stand,' the class monitor announced, 'Greet'

The class chorused 'Good morning, aunty. You are welcome. God bless you and your family. Amen!' The 'Amen' was always very loud.

'Good morning, class'

School went on smoothly that day. I had no problem with any teacher and no pupils. Beatrice and her clique did not return to disturb me. I was happy. During break, Dami, my seat mate bought me sweets. The ones that were placed on plastic sticks. They were Banana and Orange flavours respectively.

'Thank you,' I said.

'I will buy them for you every day, you hear?'

I nodded. I did not ask why he did that. I just nodded. Maybe he would be my friend. Before we went home that day, pupils were told to prepare towards the continuous assessment test, which was coming up on Friday. Fear gripped me on the announcement. The tests were what I feared the most. I wanted to fall sick. I wanted illness to be my alibi. We went home after school with a group of other students. Mama was not home when we got there. We went to her shop. Papa had gone to his friend's house to inquire about a job interview he had gone for in one of the private schools as a chemistry teacher the week before. That was what Mama told us. Mama asked us to wait in the store while she crossed to the other side of the road to buy us some food to eat. She bought us *agidi* wrapped in green banana leaves and freshly made *akara* balls. She gave us four *akara* balls each and a wrap of *agidi* each. The *agidi* was without taste as usual but we ate it all the same. I do not like it but I think Johwo likes it a lot. The *akara* balls were delicious. I relished them and wanted more. But I could not get more. Mama had prepared *Egusi* soup and *Eba*. We were having it for supper when we got home. After sending the hot *akara* balls and the *agidi* down our throats, Mama gave us sweets.

At about 5 o'clock, Mama closed the shop and we went home. There was no power supply. Mama put on the lantern and we sat down in the parlour.

'Atarhe, hope today was fine?' Mama asked.

'Mama, today was fine. I did not have any trouble.'

'Thank God.' Mama raised her hands after saying God.

Mama tied her wrapper again. I wondered why she did. It was not loosening. Maybe she did it to kill her boredom from the silence that followed her last word.

'Mama,' Johwo called.

'Yes, my child,' Mama answered.

'You didn't ask me how was school?'

Mama heaved a sigh. 'I am sorry, *biko, omote oyibo me,*' She praised, 'How was school?'

'Mama, it was fine'

'Ehen. Your father has gone to check for his new job'

'Mama, you told us. Ehn, Mama, now that Papa will work in a new place, who will now work in our farm?' I asked, worried about the farm.

'Atarhe, we will still work there'

'But, the plants, they will miss Papa'

Johwo gave a big laugh. 'Ah, Atarhe, the plants don't have eyes to see Papa or anybody'

'But, Johwo, in Elementary science we were told that they are living things,' I argued.

'Does not mean that they have eyes'

I turned to Mama. 'Mama, how could things be alive and they cannot even see?'

'Johwo, you did not explain well to your sister,' she said to Johwo. 'Atarhe, plants do not have eyes or mouth or nose or any other things that Human beings and animals have.'

'But Mama, they are alive just like human beans and animals?'

'You are correct, my child. They are alive. Just remember that. You will learn better as time goes on'

'Mama, does time go?' I asked.

Mama giggled. 'Ehn, no. I was the one who said something wrong'

'But I yam still confuse,' I said, 'Ehn, Mama, test is on Friday'

'Which Friday? This one?'

Johwo and I nodded.

'Johwo, please read with your sister starting from tomorrow. You will sleep early this night and you will start serious reading tomorrow. Read your notes and write down what you do not understand, you hear?' Mama said.

'We hear'

'Mama, I will show you the ones I don't understand. Mama...' I ran to her and held on to her wrapper. 'I yam fearing the test. I will fail again.' The last sentenced hit Mama on the head like a blow from a boxer, like Mohammed Ali. I do not know whose blow it felt like. Tears flowed down her motherly eyes and she turned away. She turned away so that I would not see them. But it was too late. I had seen them already. She loosened her wrapper, held the edge which she had tucked in to wipe her face. She tucked it back. She turned back to me. Her cheeks were tear-stained.

'*Omo me,*' Mama spoke Urhobo, 'You will not fail this time. Not this time. You will pass.'

'Mama, are you crying?'

'No, my child. Your mother is not crying. There is something inside my eye. Maybe it is dust,' she said, wiping her eyes dry with her hand.

I knew she was lying. That was certain. I had seen the tears running down, forming one wavy line on her chubby cheeks. The same chubby cheeks Johwo had. I pretended like she was saying the truth.

'Mama, don't worry. I would try and pass this time. It is third term. I have to pass,' I told her.

She smiled. Her lips curved like the edges of the hand fan on the table. She embraced me and held me in that state for almost two minutes. I was in her warm hands for some minutes and those minutes kept me away from the coldness that I felt. The coldness from the outside world. A cold, more stiffening than that of a corpse. That coldness I felt every minute of every day. It went away in those minutes. When she left me, I felt the cold return. It was there. I wanted to remain in her arms but Mama had to prepare food. She put water for *eba* in the kettle and placed it on the stove. The green stove which was covered in soot, food particles and grime. We waited for the water to boil in the parlour. Johwo sat on the blue carpeted floor and played *whot* alone. She did not say her usual 'Atarhe, let's play' and I did not ask to join her. I presumed she wanted to play alone. I sat on the wine coloured chair which had sunk inside. I could feel the wood. I sat staring at the ceiling. There was a wall gecko on it. It was a baby gecko. Certainly, it would have not spent up to four days in the world. I wonder if its mother was like mine. If she was kind and loving and protective. No, maybe the mothers of geckos abandon them to live alone, I thought.

'Food is ready,' Mama announced. She used the same words I see every day in those Mama puts and *bukas*. They wrote on their sign boards in different prints and colours.

FOOD IS READY

'Johwo! Atarhe!' she called, from the kitchen. Our kitchen was set in the corridor which opens to the backyard. It was small but it was okay for Mama, okay for us.

'Yes, Mama.' Papa warned us never to answer 'ehn' but 'yes.' He said 'ehn' was used by children with no home training. I was not dumb after all, like Papa thought. At least, I listened and I obeyed.

'Come and carry the food'

I carried the bowl of *eba* and Johwo carried the bowl that held the soup. We placed them on the coffee table and arranged three stools around it. Mama came in with a bowl of water in her hand to wash our hands. We went to fetch water for drinking in our coloured plastic cups. We placed them on the table. Mama never drank water while she ate. She always drank after eating. She only drank while eating if she was choking. I wondered maybe keeping the water till the end of the meal was her tradition or her own way of washing the food down her throat. Johwo led the grace. *'Bless us O Lord and this your gift.....'* We made the sign of the cross afterwards and washed our hands. Mama washed last and started eating. I moulded my *eba* into small fine balls and dipped into the soup and savoured the taste. I made

29

sure I ate it slowly, savouring every taste, every bit of *garri*, vegetable and *egusi*. I did not swallow lumps of *eba*. I chewed them. I enjoyed the taste better that way. I felt that I would not get the taste if I swallowed it. Moreover, I feared that the lumps would block my gullet and I would grow dumb or even worse, choke to death.

'Mama, the soup is very sweet,' I said, licking my fingers from my thumb to my pinky.

'Atarhe, say the soup is delicious not sweet. Soup can't be sweet,' Mama corrected.

'But, Mama is something that is nice in taste not sweet?' I asked.

'Yes, Mama. Is it not sweet?' Johwo also asked.

'No. Sweet is for anything that has sugar or tastes like sugar not cooked food. Things that have sugar is what you call sweet. Food is delicious,' she explained.

'Okay, Mama,' we said and continued eating.

'Mama, will you teach me how to cook it?' I asked, after the meal. I did not know how to make anything. The only thing I could do in the kitchen was to put water on fire to boil and wash the dishes. Mama looked at me and smiled.

'My daughter is growing,' she said. I smiled, my smile was rather shy.

'I will teach you, oh. *Oya,* both of you should go and wash the plates'

Papa came home just after we finished washing the plates. The lights just came on and the voltage was very high. Mama asked that we left everything off until it went down to avoid the damage of any appliance. Mama turned off the switch the fridge was connected to. Ten minutes later, the voltage steadied. The light bulb in Papa and Mama's room had blown and Papa had to change it. There was an extra 200 watts light bulb in the room. I carried one of the stools from the parlour and followed him as we passed through our narrow corridor which was no wider than the long narrow verandas in front of the classroom blocks in school. Papa was a tall man. I must have taken my height from him. He did not need more than the stool to climb. I placed the stool directly under the spot where he wanted to fix the light bulb. I did not know it would be uncomfortable for him.

'Idiot,' Papa cursed, 'Do you want me to hit the bulb with my head, instead of fixing it?'

'Papa, I put the stool so that you will climb it'

'*Ekian vwe,*' he cursed. He put his hand over his head, taking it round in the clockwise direction and snapping his thumb and his middle finger at the end of it. He arranged the stool himself.

'Stupid child. At least God should have pitied my condition and not given me a child like this. I hope when you are ripe for marriage, a good Catholic boy would find you and marry.' He shifted the stool a bit backwards, about a step backwards. He climbed and handed me the torch. 'Hold the torch properly for me,' he shouted.

Papa's words were harsh. They went through my heart like a sword piercing through it's victim. Like the swords in *David and Goliath*. I remembered the lines in the stations of the cross where Simeon told the Mother Mary that a sword would pierce her soul too. I did not cry. I could not cry. I wanted to cry badly but the tears did not come. They hid themselves in my eyes. They hid wherever they came from. I wanted them to pour exploding my pains but they did not. Papa finished fixing the bulb and we went back to the parlour. Mama had put on DRTV News. I did not enjoy news but I had no choice but to watch it.

'Papa, test is on Friday,' Johwo said. I froze. I froze like the fresh iced fish they sold in the market in cartons. The ones which had their eyes bulging out of their heads from the struggles as they froze to death in the cold rooms. Papa turned to me.

'Tarhe.' Papa never addressed me with that pet name. I was shocked. Too shocked to answer him. I just stared. I stared at his face, at his moustache which grew above his upper lip. I got my full lips from Papa. I was not just realising it but I just stared at them.

'Are you aware of the test?'

'Yes, Papa. I yam'

'I want to see your lowest score as 15 in all of the subjects. If I see 14 and below, I would deal with you in the very way you would not like. Have you heard me?' He drew his right ear to re-establish his warning.

'Yes, Papa.' The words came out in such low tone that I wondered if he heard them. He did. He heard them clearly and nodded to them.

'Papa Atarhe, don't be too hard on the girl. She will learn gradually,' Mama said.

'Gradually? *Oghene me!* Did you say gradually? Onimerire Patience Onanefe, don't make me injure you this evening. I am a Catechist and I do not want to sin against God this night,' Papa thundered.

'And treating the girl like that is not a sin to God?' Mama retorted

'Ehn?! You said what?'

'You heard me. You are a Catechist and a teacher and yet you cannot handle the responsibilities of one sick child?'

'If not for God and the fact that you are my wife, I would have beat you up today'

Mama did not say another word. Later in kitchen, I heard her mumble some words. She had gone to bring water for Papa to drink. Papa gulped the content of the cup down. I watched the movement of his Adam's apple as the water went down his gullet.

'I got the job as the Chemistry teacher in Ochuko Demonstration Secondary School,' Papa said.

'Thank God,' Mama said. 'Children congratulate your father. God is good'

'*Miguo,* Papa. Congratulations'

'*Vrendo.* Get up'

'Atarhe, Johwo. Go to bed. Pray before you sleep o,' Mama said.

'Okay, Mama.' Johwo always ran to the room with enough speed as one in a relay race. I followed her behind, walking. I knew Mama would talk to Papa. I just knew it. We never prayed alone. We always prayed together as a family. Always on every night until Mama asked us to do so this night.

'Papa Atarhe, let us talk'

'I knew something was wrong when you asked the children to go. What is it?' Papa asked like he had no idea of what Mama was asking.

'It is about our daughter, na. I don't want us to fight over her situation. Catechist, you teach children catechism. You should know that children are the greatest gifts from God to a married couple. They come in different ways as sent by God. We were not lucky enough to have a normal child as our first born but we were not so unlucky to get a handicapped child. We should encourage her and not put fear in her. The poor girl is shaken,' Mama said.

'About the test?' Papa asked, his right eyebrow rising slowly.

'Not about the test alone. About everything. She is afraid every second of her life. She fears her tomorrow. She fears that she has no place in the society. And, she fears she has no fatherly love from you. She feels cheated by her own sister. She needs your support and the confidence will come to her. I do not enjoy seeing my daughter suffer like that. I want happiness for my daughter. Let us help her, my husband. I beg you'

'I have heard you'. That was all Papa said. He added no words. He just said them plainly. Mama looked at him. Her eyes asked *Is that all?* She waited for him to say more and then stood up from her chair. 'We should pray,' she said, 'The children couldn't have started their prayers. Let me call them.' Mama came into our room. We were just getting ready to pray. 'Come let's pray,' she said. We followed her to the parlour for the prayers. Johwo again, ran back in full speed. We started the prayers with the sign of the cross, then The Lord's prayer, three Hail Marys and the Glory be. After those, Papa prayed for a safe and long happy night for us. He asked God to forgive us our sins, watch over us and wake us up happily the next morning.

Back in our room, Johwo collapsed on the bed, ready to sleep. She closed her eyes inviting sleep. I went to the table we used for reading where I usually wrote my letters. I opened my English Language notebook to the middle page and tore it out. Johwo had turned towards me.

'What are you doing?' she asked. I was startled.

'I'm not ready to sleep.' That answer was inappropriate but I gave it to her all the same.

'Okay o. You that sleeps anyhow, not ready to sleep? It is okay.'

'I said I'm not ready'

'Okay. Me, I am sleeping.' She turned and closed her eyes to sleep.

I picked up my pencil to write. It was blunt. I went to my school bag hanging on the bed and took out my sharpener. I sharpened the pencil and kept the sharpener back in the pocket of the bag where I had taken it. I did not want to misplace it. Pupils in school started using biros from primary three. Johwo had started using it already. I had to pass this term's promotion examinations to use it. Johwo never offered me her biro and I never asked for it. I went back to my seat and wrote,

Dear lettar,

I yam filled with angar, with fear, pain and bisapointment. I feel like answering my fathar dack for his wrong anb cursing way he talk to me. tobay, I bib nothing wrong but he just choose to curse me. my mama loves me a ~~plenty~~ lot, very much but Papa boes not care for me in any way. He called me idiot, stupid chilb. I cry everbay but now I bon't want to cry again. I wanted to cry this evuning but the cry bib not come. Then, I said that papa's bays of making me cry will stop. My bays of fear anb bisapointment will come to an enb. My voice will not hide again. it will reach out. I woulb not be a problem in the society but I will make a name. I will not be a wasteb chilb. Woulb not be shame among my classmates. Lettar, I will make you proub, Okay? Do you believe me? goodnight, sleep well.

Your frienb,
Atarhe

I kept the letter among the others and I went to bed. I climbed onto the bed. Johwo was fast asleep. I did not know what the next day would look like but I just slept. I had to sleep.

3

'Where is your mother?' A visitor asked. I had never seen the man before. He was a tall, young, fair man. He wore a red t-shirt and blue jeans. He had an envelope in his hand. The envelope was like the type Papa put his letters when sending them to the Priest in Rome.

'She is inside,' I answered.

'Call her for me'

I ran in. 'Mama, Mama'

Mama came out. The visitor handed her the envelope. 'That is the reply to your daughter's letters,' he said.

'Letters?'

Mama turned to me. She gave me a questioning look. I stirred and woke up. It was a dream. I yawned. I opened my mouth wide as if I was about to swallow the room. Whenever I did that in Mama's presence, she would say, '*Omo nana,* don't swallow me,' then would afterwards burst into laughter and ask me to cover my mouth. I stood up, wore my slippers and went to the kitchen where I knew I would find Mama. She was boiling water for our bath.

'*Miguo,* Mama,' I greeted her.

'*Vrendo, mome,*' she answered, 'I am boiling your water for bathing'

'Ok, Mama'

'How was your night?'

I wanted to tell her about my dream and about my letters but, 'It was fine' were the words that came out of my mouth.

'Okay, your father must have finished bathing. Let me call him so that we will pray.'

'Okay, Mama'

There was no morning Mass on Wednesday. Our prayers began with praise and worship songs. This morning I raised two worship and praise songs. At the end of the songs, Papa said, 'He who sings, prays twice.' I never knew in that saying, the word was 'prays' and not 'praise.' So I said 'praise' in place of 'prays.' It was not until the day I thought of pleasing Papa by saying the quote that I flawed. I boldly quoted 'He who sings, praise him twice.' Papa called me a deaf child asking if that was what I had been hearing them say. Mama on the other hand encouraged me. She said I did a good thing by making a trial even though I mistook the words. She added that all the same, my quote was meaningful. I never attempted saying that quote again. We read the Psalms and Canticles, and the scriptures and prayed. After prayers, Mama called Johwo and I to come and carry our bathing water. She poured hot water from the kettle into the purple plastic bucket and as she did, hot steams went up from it. I carried the bucket to the drum in the backyard which was in front of our bathroom. Our bathroom was outside, made from square shaped blue corrugated iron sheets in a square shape. We dipped the water bailer into the black drum and fetched cold water to cushion the effort of the hot water on our tender skin. About three to four people could bathe in the bathroom at once and so we both always had our baths together, splashing water on each other playfully. Mama would shout on us asking us not to waste water for whenever there was no water we had to go to our neighbour's place to fetch. They had a huge black water tank constructed high up on a red iron structure with a ladder to climb up with. I wished we had ours too. Mama would shout and shout and we would keep on playing ignoring her. I enjoyed bathing with Johwo. That was one thing I always enjoyed doing with her. That was the only time we were very sisterly. We had breakfast of *akamu* and bread. Mama bought those thirty naira worth bread from a store in the junction of our street. We rushed breakfast down our throats as Papa honked his motorcycle and called out to us.

'Where are those children? I am resuming work today, don't make me late.' Papa spoke urhobo. He mostly spoke urhobo to us whenever he was getting impatient. It was traditional of him to speak it with Mama but never with us.

'They are coming,' Mama said.

Mama had in a rush given us twenty naira note each to spend on snacks during break as she could not prepare food for us to eat. We climbed onto Papa's motorcycle. Johwo got on first before me. Mama laughed at the way I entered the motorcycle. Johwo entered the same way but

Mama said she was expected to. She said one should climb an *okada* crossing one's leg over the *okada* and not climbing on the stepper and going over before sitting on it. She would say to me 'Tarhe, you are tall like your father. Cross your legs over the *okada* and not climbing.' Papa would return 'Leave the girl alone, we are late. Let her climb as she wishes.' I wondered if Papa's reply was a sarcastic one or if he was taking sides with me or if he just wanted Mama to stop taking his time. I wanted his answer to be real. I wanted him to support me even if it was just in the case of *okada* riding. I yearned for it so much. We dropped at school and Papa drove off to his new school where he would start his work as a Chemistry teacher. I had not written my letter that morning. I decided to write it in school, during break as me and Johwo would not need to see during that time. I would stay back in class while everybody else left and write. During break, everyone went out in a rush. I stayed back and wrote.

Dear lettar,

I yam writing to you tobay from school. I bib not tell you so many things yesterbay. I was angry yesterbay.. i have not tolb you adout my frienb anb seatmate. His name is Dami. I bon't know dut he gave me two sweets yesterbay buring dreaking time. Tobay in class when aunty ask me a question that I bib not know, he tolb me the answer anb I was na able to tell aunty and she clapped for me with the class.. i like him. Lettar, are you hearing? Lettar, test is coming. I know that I will not fail Literature-in English because I have reab all the dooks and Mama explains them to me. I like literature-in-english.dut I fear Maths, English, Elementary science anb spelling anb hanbwriting. Lettar, how would I pass? What shoulb I bo to pass? My hanbwriting every test I use to get 2/10 anb most of the time is the teachers who help me, sometymes I get 1/10 and the teachars say that it is them that add the mark on top. I fear spelling a lot. You know I bon't know how to spell anb Papa says he boes not have money to buy primary dictioniry for me. if he even bougth it I bon't know if I can reab it. I yam fearing. I told Mama anb then she starteb crying. Do you know Mama was lying tobay. she was crying anb she saib she was not. Lettar, I want to pass. Senb me an angel.

Your frienb,
Atarhe

I opened the small zip at the side of my bag and kept the letter there. It was ten minutes to the end of break. I decided to take a walk. As I was about going out, when Dami came in.

'Tarhe, I did not see you outside. You did not go for the break.

'I was inside,' I answered.

'I bought you some biscuits.' He handed to me two *Noreos* biscuits.

'Thank you.' I did not know the words had slipped. 'Tomorrow will you come and watch me play football during break? Don't stay in class alone'

I did not say anything but in my silence I said yes. He understood and smiled. 'Come, let's read'

41

I smiled. 'Me? Read with you?'

He nodded. 'Don't you want to?'

'Yes, I want to. I like to'

I was glad that Dami asked that we read together. He taught me Maths. I did not understand everything he taught me but it was interesting reading with him. I prayed some of the things that we read would come out. Break had ended twenty minutes back and no teacher had come to the class. The class was noisy and the head boy from primary six came in and asked us to maintain decorum. He informed us that the teachers were summoned for a brief staff meeting. The noise died down when he came in but five minutes right after he left, the noise started again and was even worse. I told Dami that we could not continue because I would not understand anymore due to the noise. I brought my Literature book 'The Sugar Girl.' I had read it a number of times but I loved the story. Ralia's figure was a beautiful, young and spirited girl and I wanted to be like her. I placed the book on my lap holding it with my left hand. I rested my head on the desk, placing my right arm underneath it. Soon enough, I was dozing off.

School was over soon. I went to Johwo's class and we both went home as usual. There had been an accident on the way. People gathered around the scene. It was said to have been a head-on collision of two cars. They were two cars of the Toyota brand. The one coloured green was said to have been avoiding an on-coming trailer of Coca-cola products and the other was overtaking on the wrong side and both hit each other in a very drastic way. The bonnets of both cars were badly destroyed, compressed like freshly baked bread squashed by someone's hand in its hot state. I overheard one of the bystanders say that the victims had already been rushed to the General Hospital.

'I just hope that they will not die,' I said to Johwo

'Me too'

I had never seen or witnessed an accident scene before today. It was a terrible sight; quite gory. Blood stains, dried up on the navy blue tarred road in large quantity. I pictured the victims in my head. I saw them being carried, dripping of blood with their shirts soaked. They were said to have been carrying no passengers. I wondered why accidents happened but I prayed that it should not happen to my own family or to anyone I knew. I silently prayed in my heart for the victims to survive. We went to Mama's store first. She gave us the house key and told us that there was fried fish on the stove inside the covered frying pan. She asked us to soak *garri* and eat it with the fish. We told her about the accident scene.

'*Eya!,*' Mama exclaimed, snapping her fingers. 'That is bad o. I pray they recover fast'

'Yes, Mama'

'Okay, *oya* go home and eat now. I am coming in the evening'

We went straight to the kitchen on getting home. There were four pieces of fried fish and we picked out two out. One for each of us respectively. We sat and made our *garri*, as usual without milk and with two wraps of granulated sugar, one for each of us.

Johwo brought her English note and revision note and told me we were going to have dictation.

'Dictation?' I asked like I have never heard that word.

'Yes. I will give you ten words and you will spell them,' she said.

'Okay.' I went to bring my revision note from my room and my pencil. Johwo called out the words and I spelt them the way I could.

- Destiny
- Teach
- Thier
- Coluor
- Telivision
- Stop
- Dansing
- Lenght
- Soupe

I got just three right. Johwo wrote boldly on the page drawing a circle around it. She corrected the wrong spellings. She told me to stop writing both capital and small letters in the same word. I nodded. Nodded like I heard all she said. Well, I heard but I did not understand her. I picked up my elementary science notebook and started reading. I started reading it, knowing the words or not. I read. I read on. We had just Thursday before the test. I wanted to see Father Sixtus before we wrote the test. There was Mass every Thursday evening. I would see him after Mass. I read the best I could but most of the time I was just staring into space. I looked from the ceiling to the walls with their paintings peeling off into funny and awkward shapes. I wished Dami was there. I wanted him to teach me. I wanted to learn from him. He was a great teacher.

Papa came back home around six in the evening. Mama had come home by then. She served him a plate of yam and stew. She had boiled the cubed pieces of Yam and served them to him. Mama always made sure we all ate before she did. She also served us the meal and waited for us all to finish. She washed our plates and served her food. Papa told funny stories about students in his school and their characters. Mama laughed loudly. I could see her mouth wide open; lips separated, but I could not hear her voice. It seemed I had gone deaf for that moment. I stood up and said I was going to read. Papa looked at me. His look said *'I hope you read well'*

I went to my room. I made sure I closed the door that led to the corridor. I entered the room and I closed the door. I picked my school bag. I took all the books out and spread them on the bed. I picked Maths note first. I opened it. The figures were blurry. They were in my own handwriting but they seemed to be in another's. I could not see anything. It all seemed vague. I pulled out the next book and it was the same thing. I pulled the third. It was BK, Bible knowledge. It was not blurry, I could see it clearly but it was a different case with it. I stared. I stared all through holding the book in my hands. I slept off with the book in my hand. Mama came into the room later. I heard her footsteps. I did not open my eye or stir. She sat on the bed for a while. Then, she took the book from my hand and gathered the rest and put them in my bag. She patted my shoulder. *'Good night, my child.'* That was the meaning of that pat. I heard her steps leaving the room. I waited for her to go back to the parlour. I knew they were going to say the night prayers. I got out of bed, opened my bag, took out my English notebook and tore out a page from the middle again. I sat down holding my pencil. I thought of words to write but the letters and the words just came pouring out as I wrote.

Dear lettar,

Hawa you? I know you are always fine. I yam the one who always have problem. The one who is sick, sab, anb afraib. Lettar, its only tomorrow before the test. I have tryed my dest. Dami, you remeber him? He taught me tobay dut I bon't know how long I will remeber those things in my heab. They say my heab is a coconut heab. They say it is empty. They say nothing goob is insibe my heab. Johwo never says anything. Mama is the only person that speaks up for me. only Mama ever says I yam not empty. Lettar, I have reab anb reab and reab dut now I yam tried. I am tried of deing seen as a zomdie, a dullarb. A chilb without drains. I yam going to challenge God. I yam going to ask him for my miracle. I want God to tell me why he mabe me this way. I pray. I have prayeb. I have been a goob chilb to Papa and Mama. I have not fought with anydoby. I have not lieb so much. Then, what sin have I comitted that God bon't want to forgive me? papa and even fathar sixtus say that it is people ~~cho~~ who sin anb those who are wickeb that God punish. But God have punish me too.

46

God have left me to suffer and cry. Lettar, I want to ask him to please make me bettar. A lot dettar. I want him to heal me. mama says Jesus is the healer. Jesus is the healer, then let him heal me. lettar, i yam crying as I yam writing to you. I yam crying very much. I can feel the tears on my jaw. I bo not know what to bo anymore. Lettar, will I pass?

Your frienb,
Atarhe

I felt the tears on my cheeks as I dropped my pencil and folded the white paper with thin blue stripes which had my letter. They were hot. I kept the letter in the usual place and I climbed the bed and, wiping the tears. I covered myself with my cover cloth. It was a pink cloth with wine openers as the design imprinted in it. I covered myself from my head to toe and shut my eyes. I heard Johwo's heavy steps as she ran to the room. Prayers were over. Mama was asking her to go steady and not fall. I heard her voice pierce through the silence of the night. There was no power supply so the lights were out. Mama held out a torch pointing it out for Johwo. I could see the light through the open door from my wrapper. I made the sign of the cross and silently started my prayers. I said one our father, one Hail Mary, one Glory be and I shut my eyes to sleep. Johwo had jumped on the bed while I was praying. I could hear her soft breathing as she slept peacefully. She had covered herself up too. She was sleeping much more comfortably and happier than me. I wished that was me. She was a spirited

47

girl, full of life and valour. She was able to fight her battles. She was not weak and helpless like me. She had zeal. She was never lethargic about anything. I was nothing like her. We slept on till the next morning.

The next day evening, we went for evening mass. Mass on Thursday was always masses for blessings. Father Sixtus blessed items such as Olive oil, sacramentals, ornaments, kegs of water. After blessing the items, Father then asks that we all stretched out our hands with open palms. He said it was time to receive our blessings. I stretched my hands out. I wanted my blessings. Mass came to an end and I went to meet Father. He was with a number of people and I waited until he saw me and rounded up with them.

'Oke, how are you?'

'I yam doing fine, fada'

'Good, my child. Where are your mother and sister?'

'I left them inside. They are praying'

'So, what is it, my daughter? You've never come to see me alone before'

I nodded. I held my newly blessed rosary in my hand and pressed the big black beads against the skin of my palm.

'Yes?'

'Fada, tomorrow is our test'

'And you want my blessings?'

I nodded. Father Sixtus smiled. He showed his set of teeth as he did that.

'You have wisdom, my child'

'Wisdom?' I was forced to ask because I did not understand Father's view of wisdom. How could I be wise?

'Yes, you did the right thing by coming to me,' He said, still smiling. He smiled like I told him I had passed the test already. 'Let us Pray'

He laid his hands on my head and prayed. At the end, I said 'Amen'

'Thank you, Fada'

'You are very welcome. All praise to God. Write well tomorrow'

'Okay, fada.' I did not say 'I will.' I just said okay.

Papa and Mama were coming to greet Father. Johwo was in between them, holding Mama's left hand. They greeted Father and we went to the motorcycle to wait for Papa as he stayed back to speak with Father.

'Fada, I should be going now,' Papa said. He had finished discussing about the number of bags of Cement needed to complete the church compound flooring.

'Okay, Catechist'

'Okay, Fada. I should be going home now. The children have school tomorrow and so do I'

'That's true. Your wife told me. Congratulations on your new appointment'

'Thank you, Fada'

'Speaking of school, your daughter, Oke, just informed me about the test they have tomorrow'

'Yes, Fada. That's true'

'She is a bright girl. I know she will do well this term'

'Thank you, Fada'

'Enrol her for Catechism classes soon'
'Okay fada. I will'

We rode home on the motorcycle. I closed my eyes all through. The wind moved passed as we rode and I felt it. I felt its softness. I heard the trees whistling and the birds singing. I inhaled the sweetness of the air. Everything was so serene. So calm, so peaceful. And at that moment, I felt alive. For the first time, I felt my problem was coming to an end.

4

It was raining heavily that morning. It had not rained since the beginning of June. This was the 27th day and the last Friday. It was test Friday. Mama had bought me a new pencil, new eraser and a new sharpener. She did that every test and exams. She bought Johwo a new pen, pencil and eraser too. The rain was falling heavily. We would get wet if we entered Papa's bike. Papa then asked out neighbour who attended St. Andrew's with us to help him out in dropping us at school. Mr Onomuodeke, that was his name, accepted to drop us off. The weather was cold and most of the pupils were running in with umbrellas and they were drenched. The Form teachers were asked to begin the tests at 10 o' clock. Most of the pupils came in around 9.30 to 10.00 when the rain had reduced in its aggressiveness. I had written earlier on in the morning.

Dear lettar,

Rain is falling this morning and it is falling very heavy. This morning is now test morning. I hope I write well. The rain should stop or elese, we would go to school late. We will talk letar? Okay, take care.

Your frienb,
Atarhe

51

'Good luck in the test,' Chinyere said. Even though we were seatmates, we never really talked.

'Thank you. Good luck to you too'

She smiled. 'Dami has not come.'

'The rain is holding people. He will soon come,' I said.

Dami came to school 10.30am. He was lucky the test was shifted to 11 o'clock.

'Good morning'

'Good morning,' he replied.

The teacher in charge of exams and records, Mrs Ogbalor came in holding an envelope. It was brown, made of Manila paper. It was the envelope that houses the question papers. She gave them to our Form teacher and made the instructions known.

'Good morning, children,' she greeted.

'Good morning, aunty. You are wel....'

'That's okay.'

We kept quiet waiting anxiously for the instructions.

'Children, you have five questions for each subject. We have made your work easier by merging Quantitative Aptitude and Verbal reasoning with Maths and English.

Making English and Maths, eight questions each. Do you understand?'

'Yes, aunty,' we chorused

'Okay. Madam, share the questions. The duration is an hour and forty-five minutes. They start immediately you finish sharing the papers'

'Yes, ma,' Mrs Okorodafe nodded.

'Okay. Good luck children'

'Thank you, aunty'

'Good luck, Tarhe,' Dami said.

'Same to you'

I watched as Mrs Okorodafe shared the question papers turning them upside down to the blank page so that no one would see the questions before the appropriate time. The three papers stapled together as one dropped on my desk. I felt cold run down my spine. The same cold I felt all these years. The cold was back. I clenched both fists. After sharing the question papers, Mrs Okorodafe asked us to bring out our test notes and start answering. Handwriting test was to be taken after the tests printed on the question paper. I started solving the questions the way I could. Dami looked at me. He wanted to tell me the answers but we both knew the outcome of helping a friend out in exams. The teachers tagged it as 'expo.' I did not want to be tagged as an *'expo-doer.'* That was what we called them. Two hours, and forty-five minutes was soon exhausted. We submitted our papers and went out for a thirty minutes break before handwriting test.

'How did you write?' Dami asked.

'I wrote well'. I did not look at his face when he asked me and I answered still looking away.

'You are afraid of the handwriting test?'

I did not answer.

'Are you afraid, Tarhe?'

Still no response from me. He touched me slightly. I turned to look at him.

'Tarhe?'

'Leave me alone, Dami!' I walked away. I did not know why I had screamed at him. He did not deserve it. He was right. I was scared about the handwriting test but I did not want to admit it. Maybe that was why I shouted at him. We heard the *gong-gong* of the bell. Pupils ran back to their various classes. I walked. Dami was already in class. I did not look at his face. Mrs okorodafe came in holding three coloured chalks. The colours in our handwriting notes: Pink, blue, red and yellow. She also held the long metre rule which was used on the board. With the coloured chalks, she drew lines just like they were in our handwriting note. Then she wrote the sentence **The Boy Is Walking**. That was the first sentence. She drew another set of lines and wrote **I Am Dancing.** We had thirty minutes to complete the writings. The first sentence on a page and the second on another page. Dami did not look at me all through the test. I knew I had upset him. Immediately he finished writing, he submitted and left the class. When everyone had finished, Mrs Okorodafe called us all in and talked to us. She said she was sure we had all done our best and we will see our scripts by Monday. I picked up my bag and hurried out of the class the moment she released us. I wondered if I was running from Dami or the test. Johwo was already outside waiting for me.

'How was test?' she asked.

'I'm very hungry. Let's run,' I said, avoiding the question.

'Okay o. I would get home first,' she said, laughing. I did not say a word.

Papa came from school by 5 o'clock drenched to the skin. The rain had started again and this time, heavier. He hurriedly had a meal of *owho* and *starch*. There was evening mass by 6 o'clock. The rain had stopped by the time Papa had finished eating. I wore blue skirt and a white top. It was one of those skirts that Mama bought at the bend-down select. When we were ready we went to church as usual on Papa's motorcycle. There was a huge surprise waiting for us in church. Getting down from the motorcycle, we saw women and girls sweeping water out of the church at the main entrance. The rain had flooded the church compound and flowed into the church.

'Rain? *Jesu*! How did it happen?' Mama exclaimed.

'It was the water from the back of the compound that flowed into the church' one of the women tying a navy blue wrapper with a baby strapped on her back told Mama. She had spoken in Urhobo and Mama replied in Urhobo too. We went in and picked up brooms to work. Everyone was working hard to get the water out. Children like us pushed the water with the brooms. Papa rolled up his trousers and picked a broom to work. Father Sixtus who had just come in from the Parish house on seeing the scene, went back into the house. We thought he had gone to wait until church was settled for Mass but to our surprise, before our eyes, there was Father Sixtus in shorts and a white shirt. He asked Mama for broom and she went to get one.

'But Fada, you don't have to,' she said to him.

'I am young and full of life, my sister. Being a priest does not stop me from doing this. It will save time'

'Okay fada.' The work went on until Father asked us to stop and prepare for Mass.

'*Wado, o.* Thank you all. Let's prepare for Mass. Children, thank you. Gather around'

'Okay, Fada,' the children chorused. I did not say anything. I did not speak along. Mass started soon. The fans were put on to dry the terrazzo floor faster. I was dying of cold. Mama removed her upper wrapper and put it around me when she noticed I was shaking from the cold. She shifted me away from the fan. I was now sitted beside her, Johwo in the middle.

There was confession after Mass that evening as it was on every Friday evening after Mass. Mama had said earlier that she would go for it. We waited for her outside the church while Papa was talking to some men. Women and children were outside. Johwo joined the other children to play. I did not join them. I went to wait beside Papa's motorcycle making sure not to lean on it to prevent it from falling. I remembered the last time I leaned on it and it fell, how Papa scolded me and warned me never to lean on his *okada* again. Since then, I never tried it again. Mama sat in the first of the two last pews of the rows that were reserved for confession after Mass. Father then sat on a chair reserved for him by the rail where the parishioners knelt to receive Holy Communion. He wore a purple stole around his neck, different from the ones he wore during Mass. The persons for confession then went one after the other and return to the pews and pray. Papa called it Penance. I wondered what it was like telling your sins to a priest. Papa said that the priest does not keep your confession in mind but he intercedes for you with Christ. He said the priest prays and absolves your sins in the Trinity's name. I would understand better after I receive the sacrament of the Holy Eucharist. Papa came out after talking with the men. Women outside were still talking about the water that flooded into church. Mama finished her confession, said her penance and came out.

We entered the motorcycle and made for home. Papa had not asked about the test before Mass. I knew he was going to ask about it now that Mass was over. As soon as we walked through the door mat, Papa asked about the test.

'It was fine, Papa.' I made for my room after answering. I heard Papa call me back but I did not answer or turn. I heard Mama say 'Leave her, *biko*. I will talk to her. Let her be.' Papa said nothing.

The next morning was Sanitation day. Nobody was leaving the house until after 10 o'clock. Papa asked me why I walked out on him last night.

'Nothing Papa. I'm sorry.'

'Don't let it happen again. Now, eat your *akara*.' Mama had served us *akara* and bread, together with bournvita for breakfast. We ate up. At 11 o'clock, Papa went to see a friend of his. We went to the kiosk with Mama. Mama said my hair was already bushy and I needed to barb it. She said we will go to the barbing salon in our street in the evening. I was still wondering how to apologise to Dami.

'Mama'

'Yes, Tarhe'

'If you make your friend angry, how would you tell the person sorry?'

Mama smiled. 'Did you make somebody angry?'

'Yes mama. He is my friend, Dami.'

'What did you do?' she asked, still smiling. I wondered why she was smiling. 'Was it right to make a friend angry?'

'I don't know why I talked to him the way I did when he asked me if I was afraid of the test'

'What did you say?'

'I told him that he should leave me alone. Mama I was just not happy. That is why'

'It's a good thing you know you've offended your friend and you want to say sorry. Go and meet him during break time and tell him sorry'

'Will it work?'

'He is your friend, he should forgive you'

'Mama, who is that her friend, *sef*?' Johwo asked.

'You don't know him,' I sneered.

'Johwo, leave your sister to mind her business. Oya, sit down let me plait this hair'

Johwo made her hair. She usually wore thread but this week, Mama decided to make the zigzag plaits which we nicknamed *Alicia keys* after the American music star of Rock and blues star. Mama drew a small stool like the type in our kitchen and Johwo sat on it. I handed the wooden cutting comb to Mama and she got to business. The plaits were nicely made, not too tight and not loose either. Mama had crafty hands in hair making. I wanted to make my hair too but Mama thought it wise for me to have it cut. She rounded up the hair do in another one hour and thirty minutes. It was beautiful, bringing out Johwo's beautiful, round and fair face.

'Johwo, your hair is fine,' I said.

'Thank you. Mama is a good hair plaiter,' she said.

'Johwo, hair-doer or maker, not plaiter,' Mama said.

'Okay Mama is a good hair maker'

'Good,' Mama applauded. 'You children must be hungry.'

'Mama, yes o. My belly is doing gru-gru,' Johwo said, trying to mimic the sound of her rumbling stomach. Mama laughed.

'It is doing gru-gru? Ah, this girl ehn. Okay let's go home and warm the *owho* and boil yam for you to eat with it'

'Okay, mama.' Mama locked the kiosk and we followed her. She heated up the soup and boiled the yam. We ate, talked and talked. I was anxious about Monday. I wanted it to come soon so I will apologise to Dami.

As I wished, Monday came soon. I woke up, earlier than usual. I suppose I must have woken at the first crow of the rooster. I sat down to write the day's letter.

Dear lettar,
Tobay is the bay I yam going to tell Dami that I yam sorry for shouting at him. Do you think that he will forgive me? i yam praying he forgives me or elese I will cry in his front. He shuolb forgive me. I bon't even know why I shouteb at him. It was a mistake. I know I

59

will not bo it again. Dami is a goob frienb. I will try not to make him angry again. I will try not to shout at him again. we start seeing test scripts tobay. I want to pass. I hope I pass. I woulb tell you more about it when I come back from school. Byebye.

Your frienb,
Atarhe

Morning prayers were said; breakfast of yam and warm stew was had and we were afterwards dropped at school. Dami was not in class. Chinyere said he had gone to buy a new pencil. I waited for him. Dami came just in time before the teacher entered. We said nothing to each other. We were having Maths first and Mrs Okorodafe had brought out our test notes which were already marked. I could hear my heart beat. It was the same sound that I heard from Mama pounding food substances in the mortar - the sound of the *pow, pow, pow* of the pestle striking. Mrs Okorodafe asked the class monitor to share the books to us. I opened my book slowly and turned it page after page - Maths 5, English 7, BK 12, Elementary science 10, Health Education 12, Urhobo 13. I was waiting for the handwriting book to be passed. I scored 2. My test scores though poor were a huge improvement for me. I closed both books and kept them in my school bag. Classes started. In each subjects the test corrections were done and I wrote them down to study when we got home.

Break time bell was rung and we all ran out as usual. Dami had gone out before me. He was headed for the Mama put cart where *banga,* jollof and white rice, beans, spaghetti are sold. The lady usually placed her cart by the classroom blocks selling to both students and teachers. After he bought his *banga* rice tied in a transparent cellophane bag, he went to sit on the bench under the big mango tree by the side of the classroom blocks. He started eating from the hole he had made in the water proof bag. I walked up to him. He saw me coming. I knew he did but he pretended not to. He continued savouring his meal. I went to the bench and sat down, making sure I left space enough for another person to sit in between us.

'Hawa you?' I asked. He did not turn to look at me nor did he answer. He was doing exactly what I had done to him. It was payback time.

'Dami, I yam sorry na,' I said. I moved closer and touched his right shoulder. I expected him to shout at me just as I did to him. Instead, he said nothing. He kept on eating. The rice smelt nice.

'Is the food sweet, ehm, delicious?' I asked, remembering what Mama had taught Oke and myself. It was a stupid question, quite uncalled for. I compared myself to Peter during the transfiguration who asked to make three booths for Jesus, Moses and Elijah.

'Atarhe, leave me na,' he said.

'Dami, please na. I was angry so I just shouted.' He looked at me with those eyes that looked like the ones a judge gave to an accused in court. I wondered if he wanted to tell if I was lying or saying the truth from my eyes. He smiled.

'I'm not angry again. You want rice?' he asked.

'No, I don't want. Thank you.'

He smiled. He finished up the rice in the water proof package and threw the wrap on the floor. School was littered with those wraps.

'So.....Dami, I did not really pass well but it is better,' I said.

'That's better. I saw the scores.'

'How?'

'Did you say how? We are on the same seat'. He laughed. 'You thought being angry with you will stop me from checking on you? You are my friend.'

I smiled. 'Thank you'

'Your parents would be happy that you improved even just a little.' He said.

'I hope Papa understands that'

'Why are you saying so?'

The bell rang. 'Let's go to class. Let's run. I will gap you,' I said.

'Okay, try me.'

We raced to class. Dami got the lead and we laughed over it when we got to class. It was a funny race. I wondered how I would show the scores to Papa. Mama was sure to smile and tell me 'Tarhe, you did well, you would do better.' We got home, had lunch and watched cartoons as we wanted for Papa to come so that we would tell him our test scores. Papa came home and he ate. After, Johwo had carried the plates away. I dropped the bomb.

'Papa, test results have come'

'Oh, ehen, okay bring it. Let me see,' he said.

I handed the book to him. He asked me to go and bring his glasses. He had it pinched on his nose. Papa rolled his eyes as he flipped through the note, page after page. Mama sat on her chair waiting anxiously for him to pass the notebook to her.

'And handwriting?' Papa asked, raising his head up from the book. He asked about the handwriting note without commenting on the results he had seen. I feared the worst was about to happen. I knew Papa was piling them up in his mind to give an outburst at once. I handed the handwriting note. He looked at it. Then, he raised his eyes from it and looked at me. He passed the note to Mama.

'See what your daughter spends my sweat on. Johwo, let me see your notes'

Mama flipped through the notes. 'Ah, Papa Atarhe, Atarhe did a lot better than last terms tests. This time, she improved in her health education, elementary science and even her English. Last year it was 2. She tried'

Papa looked at Mama disgustingly. 'Tried? Today I know you and your daughter are both sick in the head.' He threw Johwo's notes at Mama. 'See what a better child has done'

'I will be a better child,' I mumbled.

'*Die?* What did you say?'

'I said I too can be a better child'

'Atarhe the dreamer. Keep dreaming.' Papa stood up and went to his room.

'Johwo you did very well. Tarhe you are coming up. Well done, my children.' She gave us a big hug. I smiled.

For the first time, Papa's words did not hurt me. They were like a driving force for me. My good days were yet to come. My night's letter was beautiful and happy.

Dear lettar,
Hawa you? I yam so so happy. I fill fulfiled. Do you know that for the first time, Papa's worbs bib not make me sad. It mabe me feel that I can de dettar. I yam dettar. Do you know Mama saib that I mabe dettar scores than defore. It is a miracle. The scores are low dut with help anb more effort, I will de dettar. Lettar, tobay I say to you. I, Atarhe Okeoghene Onanefe will de a dettar girl. Good night.

Your frienb,
Atarhe

I had a sound night rest. There was this feeling. I think it's what they call butterflies.

5

School was different that morning. Mrs Okorodafe was not in class. The head teacher, Aunty Rachel informed us that a new teacher was coming to our class as our form teacher. Mrs Okorodafe had been transferred to another school somewhere in Olomu. By 8 o'clock, the new teacher, Miss Mary-Rose Ogbalefe came into the class. She was a young woman, possibly in her mid twenties. She was beautiful, dark-skinned, tanned skin like the colour of the Cadbury chocolates Father Sixtus bought for us anytime he travelled. Her eyes were light brown and almost seemed like they were artificial contact lens. She was in a khaki trouser and jacket with a white polo having some kind of logo drawn on it. It was the uniform of the National Youth Service Corps. She was a youth corps member. It was no wonder she was young. She introduced herself to us and asked for our names. Her voice was beautiful and quite sonorous. I was sure she could sing beautifully. Her voice sent out this message to the class, to me. I hoped to like her. I knew she was different from all the other teachers who had taught us. She smiled brightly exposing a beautifully arranged set of teeth. They shone like the ones of the persons in close up toothpaste commercials.

'How are you, children?' she asked, after introducing herself to us.

'We are fine, thank you aunty,' We chorused.

'Let's do a little morning exercise. It is a warm up, okay?'

'Okay, aunty'

'Now, how many of you know the song, if you are happy and you know?'

'I, aunty.' Voices from different directions with hands raised up were heard and seen.

'So the response is?'

'Clap your hands,' the class chorused.

'Good! Absolutely wonderful,' she smiled cheerfully 'So, let's sing'

She started the song and we joined her in the singing, clapping our hands, stamping our feet, saying the name Jesus and so many other gestures as the song required. It was fun. After the song, she let us sit down and rest for a little while and then asked us for our notes.

'Girls and boys,' she called out, smiling.

We were quiet. We sat mute like people who were not being addressed and were busy with their businesses.

'Children, when I say boys and girls, you say 'Yes, aunty.' Is that okay?

'Yes, aunty'

'Boys and girls,' she called out again.

'Yes, aunty,' we answered. I was excited. I liked her.

'Very good. Please submit your notes to me. Any subject at all. Place them on my table'

We hurriedly went to the table to submit our notes one after the other creating a little noise as we stood up from our seats pulling chairs and desks. We laid the books one on top of the other. All books were kept closed. We only left the books open when there was a homework for marking. After the submissions, we went back to our seats.

'Settle down, children. Thank you. Now, I want you to open to Unit 4 in your English reader.' She waited for us to open our text books to the unit. 'Is everybody there?'

'Yes, aunty,' we answered.

'Okay, read the passage, underline new words, answer the questions on a sheet of paper. This is not a single work. You are working with your seatmates. So, pick one person who would write for your seat. I am giving all of you thirty-minutes.'

We told Chinyere to write for us. She had a legible writing, visible and beautiful. While we read, Miss Mary-Rose went through our notes. She put some on the right and others on the left. I figured the ones on the left to be like the unjust which God would not accept as in the Bible and the ones on the right, the righteous which were God's people. It was like placing the books into castes like in human societies; the rich and the poor, the unclean and the accepted. I just kept on wondering what she was doing.

'Tarhe,' Chinyere called, 'You are not even joining us to read'

'Sorry. Let us read'

We wrote down our answers, each person contributing answers. When it was time to submit, Chinyere submitted for our group. Miss Mary-Rose asked for our class monitor and Nyerohwo went to her. She gave her the notes to share.

'Open your notes and see what I wrote on them,' she said.

She had written in our notes in red ink which was the teacher's colour of pen ink. Some had good comments. In clear writing I saw the words **'See me, Atarhe.'** I hoped I was not in trouble.

'If you have 'see me' on your book. Come during break'

Dami had a good remark but he had circles on so many pages for no date. I always wrote my date. I never forget to write my dates. Chinyere had 'wonderful' written on her notes.

During break, four of us who had been asked to see the teacher went to meet her. She asked the first three people to come and she showed them their mistakes and faults. She asked them to go outside and play after talking to them. Then, I went forward to meet her.

'Aunty, good morning'

'Morning, dear. You are Atarhe Onanefe?'

'Yes, aunty'

'Sit down.' I sat on the second chair like the one she sat on.

'Tarhe, how old are you?' she asked. I was quiet. This same old question but it sounded different, really different. It sounded softer, sounded more peaceful. I wanted to answer but the words hung tight at my lips. I heard her ask again.

'My dear, how old are you?'

This time I answered. 'I yam ten years old'

'Say it again,' she said.

'I yam ten years old'

'No, darling. It is I am not, I yam. Now, say I am ten years old'

'I yam.... am ten years old,' I said.

'Don't worry you would learn it soon enough, okay?' I nodded. She was a comfortable person to talk to. She had a great charisma and a cheerful countenance.

'Atarhe, your handwriting and spelling is one of your major problems. You are very poor in handwriting and you have spelling problems. Do you practice?'

I bowed my head low. I did not answer.

'Tarhe, don't be afraid, Okay? I am your teacher and I am here to help you. Is that okay?'

'Yes, aunty'

'Okay, I want you to go home and write me a composition on the topic 'My Father'

'Okay, aunty'

'Okay, write it on a sheet of paper and submit it to me when we come to school tomorrow. We really need to work on your handwriting and spelling.'

'Thank you, aunty'

'Okay, go out for break.' Just then, the bell rang. 'Oh, sorry my dear'

'Thank you, aunty,' I said again.

'Wait, you did not buy break biscuit?'

'Yes, aunty,' I answered, nodding.

She smiled. 'You'd say 'No, aunty'

She brought out a packet of coaster biscuits from her black bag which was under the teacher's table. She gave it to me.

'Here, eat this one'

'Aunty....'

'Take it, *jare*. Eat,' she insisted.

'Thank you, aunty'

I went to my seat and waited as the whole class came in and settled down. I had eaten the biscuit before Dami and Chinyere came in. Everyone settled for the rest of the day's classes. I liked Miss Mary-Rose. I just liked her. I saw her as God's sent gift to us in the class, especially to me. She must be the Angel I asked for in my letter. I just knew it. I felt it. She reminded me of my homework after school that day. She did not give us any general homework being her first time of coming in as our class teacher. Johwo came to my class and we both went home. Mama did not go to the shop that morning. She had complained of fever and had stayed back at home. By the time we got home, she was feeling better. She even looked better. She said she had eaten, taken some drugs and gone to sleep.

'Thank God,' Johwo said.

'Hope school was fine?' Mama asked.

'Mama...'

'Mama, they gave us a new aunty in my class,' I said, interrupting Johwo.

70

'Yes, Mama. Primary 2 was given a new teacher,' Johwo said. Perhaps to talk just to show that I had no right to interrupt her.

'Hmmmm, hope she is a good teacher?'

'Mama, she is very nice. She said she would help me with my handwriting and spellings and all my other problems'

'That's wonderful,' she said, 'Come, let me give you your food'

There was boiled plantain and stew in the kitchen for us to eat. Mama served for us in one plate and put a piece of meat which she tore into two with her teeth for us. After lunch, Johwo sat down to watch Tom and Jerry. I told Mama I was going to read inside. I went to the room, closed the door and sat down to write my letter.

Dear lettar,

I ~~yam~~ am very happy tobay. school drought a new ~~lettar~~ teacher for us. Her name is aunty Maryrose. She is a youth corper. You know all those people that have finish university anb are now wearing all these uniforms. She is deautiful and very frienbly. Do you know that she even saib that she will help me to correct all my mistakes anb teach me well so that I can pass well. Lettar, aunty Maryrose is a nice woman. She is caring. Ehen, she even gave me discuit to eat buring dreaking time. I like her alreaby. I pray that they bo not transfer Mrs Okorodafe. Me, I like aunty Maryrose. When you see her, you will like her too. Even more than me. she saib that I shoulb write a composition on my father. Lettar, I bon't know what to write insibe that composition. I will write the truth. The truth adout my relation

71

with papa. Lettar, I yam just happy. She is now my third frienb after you decause there is you, Dami anb aunty Maryrose. Let me go anb bo the homework.

Your frienb,
Atarhe

I had a smile on my face as I dropped the pencil and folded the paper. My eyes crinkled as I smiled. I was not sure I had smiled that much in a long time. My prayers were gradually being answered by God. The smile did not want to go off my face even when I wanted it to. I wrote the composition. I was still smiling. Gradually, it faded away. I wondered if it faded away because I was writing about Papa. I wrote about Papa describing him physically and also by his actions. I heaved a sigh of relief as I finally finished writing the composition. I looked at the handwriting. I shook my head. It looked ugly. I took out another sheet of paper and re-copied it into the plain sheet. I wrote it this time more slowly and carefully trying to make the writing a bit clearer. I wished my handwriting was like Chinyere's. It would have been much better. I left the paper which I wrote the composition in my English notebook and kept my letter in the bucket under the bed as usual. I went to the parlour. There was still power supply. The Mexican soap opera which aired every weekday evening at 4 o'clock was just about to start. I did not always watch except when I walk into it and even then, I do not understand the concept of the story. They were too technical, too mature for me. Mama enjoyed watching them.

The one showing was about a young girl who was brought up by an old couple in a village. The couple had found her by the waterside close to their shack. They brought her up and told her that they are her grandparents but she is indeed the daughter of a wealthy man. The story was something of that nature. I sat down to watch with Mama and Johwo. Mama talked and commented at every single speech of every character, Male to Female, Lords to maids, like she was the Director of the series.

'Mama,' Johwo called.

'What?'

'Do you want to enter the television?'

I heard myself laughing. I laughed out so loud that I felt my body heave with it. It felt good.

'Ehn, What is it? Why are you laughing. You are seeing the girl entering trouble and you say that I should keep quiet'

'Mama, if you talk, it will not change the movie. There will be no difference,' Johwo said.

'Ehn, leave it like that. You small rats want to use me your mother for your joke ehn'. She laughed too. She was happy. Johwo was happy. I was happy.

School was the next morning. We went to bed early after night prayers as led by Papa. The next morning, Mama made breakfast for us and put food in our flask for us to take to school. I submitted the composition to Miss Mary-Rose. She was punctual. She was already in school by 7.30am, a whole thirty more minutes before assembly. During break, she called me to see her. Johwo was waiting for me outside. I sent word through Dami to tell her to eat and keep the rest for me since I was with my teacher.

'Atarhe, your composition is interesting. So, your father is a catechist?' she asked. I had written that in the composition.

'Yes, aunty,' I nodded as I answered. Perhaps just saying yes was not enough.

'Good. I am a Catholic too'

'Okay.' I did not know what else to say.

'Tarhe, I want you to go out for break now. So that you can go out for break now, I want you to write for me the Capital letters and Small letters of the alphabet. The capitals should be the first you'd write and then the small letters will be under them. Do you understand?'

'Yes, aunty'

'Okay, you can go for a break'

I went out to meet Johwo in front of her class. She had finished eating. I collected the food left from the flask. I told her that I was sorry, that teacher kept me back. She ran along to play with her friends in the field. Community Primary School's field was big enough for the boys to play ball and the girls to play ten-ten all at the same time without confusion. I saw Dami under the same Mango tree he had sat under the day I apologised to him. We shared my food. The spoon Johwo used was in the flask and I gave it to him to eat with. It was coconut rice. That was Mama's favourite. We finished it just in time before the usual *gon-gong-gong* of the bell was heard.

'She likes you,' Dami said, as we walked to class after break.

'Who?' I asked, dazed.

'Aunty Mary-Rose'

'Oh'

'That is why she has been calling you every breaking time.' He said it with all confidence as though he read Miss Mary-Rose's mind. As if he was so sure that she liked me.

'I don't know if she likes me but I like her. I like her very much. She is caring like my Mama,' I told him.

'What do you do every breaking time?' he asked, curiously.

'She use to check my notes and give me work to do especially on spelling and handwriting'

'She must be a nice aunty then', he said.

'Yes, she is'

We sat down in class. The class was not noisy today. Everyone was quiet and of good conduct. Miss Mary-Rose had her ways of teaching that made the whole class like her.

Good news awaited Johwo and I at home. Mama was pregnant. It was six weeks old. That was the reason for her recent fevers in the morning. Papa had not come back and so Mama told us not to speak of it to him when he comes. She intended it to be a surprise for Papa. She had prepared *Ukodo* with the things she brought from the market. Papa came home to meet this august meal. He smiled at Mama.

'Onimerire, what is it?'

'What?'

'You are up to something'.

'Ah, Ah. Papa Atarhe why would I just start planning a coup on your head? Please, eat the food let the children wash the plates.'

Papa ate the food relishing every bit of it. From the yam, to the unripe plantain, the pepper soup and red oil. After he finished the meal, I brought water in the green bowl meant for washing hands. I also brought a table napkin. It was red in colour with a memorial print on it. It must have been one of those Papa brought from a burial ceremony. Papa washed his hands in the bowl and dried them with the napkin.

'Now, Onimerire tell me the truth. We only have *ukodo* once in a while in this house. What happened that you made it for us to eat o?'

'Okay o. Since you do not believe that I cannot make food for you without being up to something, I will tell you what you want to hear,' Mama said.

'Ehen! I said it that you people knew something. What is it?'

She smiled. 'I am six weeks gone.' I wondered if that meant pregnant or something else. Perhaps, she was telling Papa something first before she would say she was pregnant. Then, I saw Papa in his tall self stand up from his seat and raised his hands up to the ceiling. 'Thank God. *Oghene me, do,*' He said. He embraced Mama warmly and praised her. I was happy. I was sure it was going to be a boy this time. I just felt it. It was a boy. And, I would name him Oghenemudiaga and we will call him Mudiaga. I did not

76

say my thoughts out. I just conceived it. I would let them out when Mama was almost due for delivery. That night we said night prayers happily and went back to our rooms. Papa prayed a long prayer for Mama's safety and the safety of the unborn child and keeping our family whole and happy. Papa also told me that from next week Monday I was going to attend catechism classes. I was happy when he said that. I did not smile or talk or even say 'Thank you, Papa.' Rather, I just stared at Papa who was smiling at the good news he had received.

Johwo had homework and so did I. We sat at the reading table to do our homework but we discussed about our unborn sibling instead of doing our work.

'Tarhe, he will be a fine baby,' Johwo said.

'Yes, he will be. I know that it is a boy. Papa have been saying boy boy boy since. This is the time God has destined to bring the boy to our house,' I said.

'Yes. That's why Mama and Papa use to say that God is good.'

Johwo started writing her homework but I stared in the direction of the door. She did not ask about my homework or why I was staring, she just kept on writing. She finished before I thought of starting mine.

'You have been looking at the door since. I am going to sleep. Good night,' she said.

'Good night. Dream of baby'

She laughed. 'Don't worry. I will dream plenty. Stop looking and write your homework.'

I was feeling sleepy already I had to do the homework and write my letter. I picked my pencil and scribbled the letters in the last page of my English notebook. I tore out a sheet for my letter.

Dear lettar,
Do you know how happy I yam, aunty say is am., not yam, bo you know how happy I am now? Mama just saib that she is preginant. My Mama is preginant anb I know she will dorn a dady doy. The doy that Papa have been waiting for all these many years. I know that you are happy for me anb for Mama. Lettar, they will now de calling Mama babuwa. I am laughing. It is a nice feeling. I will tell Dami and Miss Maryrose tomorow. God dless my Mama. Bless my dady for us. Amen.

Your frienb,
Atarhe

The next day was brighter than every other day I had had in my life as far as I could remember. The air smelt nice with the blend of the morning dew and the dust from the earth after the rain. It had rained the night before but the dullness and coolness of the weather did not ruin the day but made it brighter in my eyes. I wanted to smile all day, my smile brighter than the *Close up* commercials, brighter than I had ever done. Papa dropped us at school and gave us money additional to the one Mama had already given us. Papa was indeed happy. It was clear in his behaviour. I was happy. We were all happy.

'Good morning, aunty. You are welcome. God bless you and your family. Amen,' We greeted Miss Mary-Rose as she entered the class, saying the words slowly. She asked us to bring out our Maths note and place them open on our tables. She wrote some questions on the board for us to solve. Dami was helping out in the first question when Miss Mary-Rose walked to our desk and asked us to change positions. She asked Chinyere to come to the middle while Dami sat in Chinyere's position. She asked us to submit when we were through. Soon, the whole class were through with the classwork and everyone was submitting. I was not sure what my score would be. By the time we got our notes back I was surprised to see 3/5 written on the page. I had written well.

'Class, when I give you class works or tests, I do not want people working together. You are meant to do it yourself. Is that clear?' Miss Mary-Rose said.

'Yes, aunty,' we answered.

'Atarhe, see me during break'

I went to her during break.

'Where is the note? The letters?' When she said letters for a moment, I thought she meant my letters and I wondered how she found out about them. 'Atarhe, the assignment on the alphabets'

'Okay, aunty.' I went to my seat to bring them. 'Sit down, Tarhe'

She opened the note and went through the letters. 'Come, Atarhe.' She held out an outstretched arm for me to hold and drew me to her side of the table gently. 'Can't you see the problem, Atarhe?' She picked a pencil from her desk and asked me to write the small letters b and d. I wrote d for b and b for d. 'You see, one of your problems is in inter-changing the two letters. You are good with the capital letters but the small letters are your problem. Your small letter z is like the number 3. And, in your composition, I noticed that you write both small and capital letters together.'

I nodded.

'Does anybody teach you at home?' she asked.

'My Mama, sometimes. My sister is in primary 3 but she does not have time always'

'And your father?'

'My Papa does not really like me. He calls me a dullard child. Aunty, I yam always afraid to talk to him. Only Mama loves me a lot.'

'Hmmmm,' she sighed. 'I love you too, Atarhe. I love all my pupils.' I want the best for all of them including you. We will get help, don't worry. You will pass this class and every other class'

'Thank you, aunty'

'You are welcome. Now, go on and play'

'Aunty, my Mama is preginant,' I said.

'Wow. That's good news.'

'Yes, aunty'

'And, it is pregnant not preginant,' she corrected. I smiled and went out to play.

6

Miss Mary-Rose had insisted on coming to visit Mama and Papa and talk to them about my performance in school. I had given her the address, describing the way to the house. She came on Saturday morning. We had just finished breakfast when she came. Papa was not going out till in the evening. Mama and I, together with Johwo would go to the farm later in the afternoon. Breakfast was hot yam porridge which Mama prepared. It was very tasty. The yellowish sauce together with the slices of yam settled on my taste buds without discomfort. I enjoyed every bit of it. I had just finished washing the plates when the knock on the door was heard.

'Atarhe,' Mama called, 'Go and check the door. Somebody is knocking'

'Okay, Mama.' I opened the door and saw Miss Mary-Rose standing there in a black pair of jean trousers and a yellow sleeveless top with a black collar. She had her hair made in the style called Bob Marley, after the Rastafarian musician who was on dreadlocks in his time. She let the braids fall down on her slender shoulders.

'Mama, it is Aunty in my school'

'Oh, let her in,' Mama said.

I gave way for her to come in. She greeted Mama and asked about Papa's whereabouts. Mama offered her a chair.

'Yes, my husband is at home. Sit down, my sister. Tarhe, go and tell your father that your teacher is here.' I went inside to call Papa. I heard Mama tell Johwo to take two hundred naira from her black purse and go to one of the nearby stores and buy a soft drink for Miss Mary-Rose.

'Ah, no ma. There's no need for that. I just ate before coming and will be going to a friend's birthday party later on today. I am fine. Thank you'

'Ehen, okay.'

Papa came in. He held in his right hand a Vanguard newspaper. The newspaper of the day before. He had his glasses on.

'Ah, my sister, Welcome. What can I do for you?,' he asked.

'Good morning, sir. I am Miss Mary-Rose Ogbalefe. Atarhe's class teacher,' she said, introducing herself.

'The new one? I did not know you were this young,' Papa said.

Miss Mary-Rose laughed lightly. 'I am a youth corps member, sir'

'Okay. That is nice. Where are you from?'

'I am from Agbara. But, I schooled in Ife. Obafemi Awolowo University.,' she said.

'Oh, great Ife people. My friend stayed there with some white men that were lecturers then. The school is a very beautiful place. Welcome, you are welcome'

'Thank you, sir. I am here because of Atarhe,' She said.

'Obviously. So, my sister, what is it about the girl that brings you to my home?'

I sat on the chair opposite Papa. He looked at me and I shifted unsteadily, trying to move away from being directly opposite him.

'I discovered your daughter's slow performance in and outside class. I want us to sit and talk about the problems that are causing this poor performance in her school work.'

'Ehen. Thank you. So, what are these problems,' Papa asked.

'I noticed some major issues in her handwriting and spellings'. She turned to me, 'Tarhe, please go and bring your English notebook' I went to the room to get the note.

'Sir, your daughter has the zeal to learn but she is physically challenged with what I think is a brain disorder or mental retardation. She is very timid, shy and also naive. She finds it hard to understand little things. She is slow to comprehend and afraid to try new things'

'Yes. Yes, that's very true.' Mama said, shifting on her chair.

I came back with the note in my hand. Miss Mary-Rose collected the notebook from me and opened it to show Papa and Mama who were sitting together on the sofa.

'I have circled her problems in red ink. You would see that she usually mistakes the small letters b and d for each other. I also noticed this and gave her a composition to write. I have the composition in my drawer circled with these mistakes'

'So, what are you saying we should do?' Papa asked.

'I want us to work actively to help her. She said nobody has the time to tutor her except you, ma, when you return from your shop. I don't know how we would resolve this but we all need to put our heads together and help her in correcting her mistakes.'

'Now, my question is how are we going to correct this problem?' Papa asked.

'Sir, I do not know what you think of a special school. She would really need the help of one. They handle cases like this. As it is, she is already ten and lagging where are age mates are'

'Special school? I am just a catechist and a part time teacher. My wife is pregnant and I do not have money to place a child in a special school. Moreover, there are no good ones in this area. I can't consider that option'

'Then sir, we should at least check her IQ and if possible check for any mental illness that could be the cause of this. Then, we will know how well to handle her condition'

'I think you are right,' Mama said.

Papa cleared his throat. 'Ehn, what is that your name again?'

'Mary-Rose,' she answered.

84

'Yes, Mary-Rose. Are you a Catholic?' Papa asked. I wondered if that question was necessary.

'Yes, sir. I was born and brought up as a Catholic'

'Very good. In the name of Jesus and our blessed virgin Mary, don't come to my house and tell me how to raise my child. I have a family where I am the head and I know how to take care of them. I do not need little girls who have not even married to advise me'

'Sir?'

'Yes?'

'I just want you to consider the pain of your daughter. She cries everyday because she thinks she is lacking your fatherly love which she wants so badly. She did not make herself like this. Moreover, she is not an imbecile. You cannot handle an imbecile. God made her like this for a purpose,' Miss Mary-Rose said.

'Papa, Atarhe. Please, hear her out,' Mama said.

Papa shot a cold look at Mama. 'Better hold your peace there'

'Okay, o'

I sat saying nothing. I sat there watching the lips of each individual as they moved. I concentrated on the lips as though my life depended on them. As if I would see the words as they are pronounced out of the lips. Johwo sat still, looking at me from time to time. I did not ask why. It was not her fault. She had the right to look at me as much as she wanted.

'And Miss youth corper. You are not a member of my family. You are my teacher's daughter and your work stays in school not in my house. The government pays you for that. Teach her and stay out of me and my family's matters. Don't tell me what to do with this child,' Papa said.

'Okay, sir. It is not a matter of quarrel. I would be going now. Atarhe, I will see you in school on Monday. Take care,' Miss Mary-Rose said, standing up from her seat.

'Yes, aunty,' I said.

'Tarhe, see your teacher off to the road. My sister, Thank you,' Mama said.

'Sit down. I will close the door after her,' Papa said.

I stood up and went to my room. I started crying. The tears came running down without control. I saw them drop on my pillow as I laid my head on it. I wiped them off my face. I stood up, went to the reading table and tore out a middle page off my English notebook. I was running out of middle pages. I heard Johwo's footsteps. I closed the notebook with the torn out paper in it. I rested my head on the table.

'Mama is calling you,' she said.

'Where is Papa?'

'He has gone out'

I did not hear when Papa went out. The sound of his *okada* must have drowned in my tears.

'Tell Mama that I yam coming,' I said.

I went to meet Mama. She sat me down and told me a few things about hope, patience and faith. She said that I should not worry that things would change. I nodded. I made to go back to the room to write my letter. Johwo turned to me and said.

86

'Tarhe, don't worry. I hope things will get better too. I nodded. I wanted to smile. I could feel it that I wanted to smile but my lips were still. They did not turn upwards. They just kept still. I went to the room. I sat down and I wrote.

Dear lettar,

Tobay Aunty Maryrose came to my house. She came to see Papa and Mama this morning. she was telling them that I neeb help in so many ways. I know Mama unberstanbs. But papa boes not want to understanb. I bon't know anymore. Johwo is also a caring sistar. Now I know that she likes me. I wanteb to smile at her. To tell her thank you dut I coulb not. Aunty was correct. I am too afraib to talk or bo what I want to bo. I fear too much. I only have no fear when I talk with you. you are my goob frienb. I just want this problems to enb and answers to come to me. I yam happy that aunty came to see me. I told you defore, she is like Mama.

Your frienb,
Atarhe

I did not do anything that Saturday. I slept through most of it. Mama understood. She went to the farm with Johwo.

Sunday homily spoke to me. Father Sixtus said that someone would receive his or her miracle in the church. He said that the cries of that person have been heard and God understands the person's pain. When he said that we should raise our hands and receive our blessings. I did. Mama prayed silently by my side with her lips moving fervently just like Hannah in the Bible. I knew she had me in her prayers. I prayed also.

Miss Mary-Rose was not ready to give up on me. She came again to see Mama after school on Monday. I had to go with Johwo to catechism class by 4 o'clock. Mama was in the shop. I took her there to meet Mama

'Ah, Aunty Mary-Rose. You came today?'

'Yes, ma. I came to seek your permission to allow me keep Atarhe till 4 o'clock every day. I hope you agree. I will like to teach her some things privately,' she said.

'This lady,' Mama smiled. 'You are too kind. God will bless you with all you want,' Mama said.

'Thank you, ma,' Miss Mary-Rose smiled, 'So, is that a yes?'

'Yes, but on Mondays like this and Fridays, she will close normally because she has Catechism classes'

'Okay, no problem, Ma. Thank you.'

'Alright, my sister'

'I should be leaving now, Ma. Ehen, I forgot to congratulate you on your pregnancy the other day. Congrats, ma,' Miss Mary-Rose said, getting up. She brushed her white and black striped skirt with her right hand.

'Thank you, my sister. Okay, Johwo and Atarhe greet aunty for me and say bye-bye,' Mama said.

'Thank you, aunty. Bye-bye,' We said.

'Okay, children. See you in school tomorrow'

'This your teacher is very nice, o,' Mama said, when she had gone.

'Yes, Mama. I like her very much', I said.

'She's good. Many people like her in school,' Johwo added.

Johwo and I went home to prepare for Catechism. There was evening Mass. We greeted Father Sixtus before leaving after Mass.

'Hmmm, my daughter is now attending Catechism classes o,' He said.

I smiled, without showing my well arranged and sparkling set of teeth. 'Catechist, thank you for allowing her to be part of this,' Father said, turning to Papa

'We have to do what we have to do as parents in the Catholic church,' Papa said, smiling. I wondered why he was taking the credit. Mama looked at him with eyes full of accusations. It was her pregnancy not his idea that made him enrol in the class.

'Fada, I want you to bless my Mrs,' Papa said, 'She is pregnant'

'Wow! So these little girls especially this little Johwo will be big sisters, ehn?' He laughed. 'God is good. Let us pray'

He laid his hands on Mama's head and prayed for her and the baby, and also for the whole family.

'God bless you. Take care, Madam,' He said, at the end of the prayer.

'Thank you, Fada,' Mama said.

'Our able Fada. Thank you,' Papa added.

Father Sixtus laughed. 'Catechist, you and your funny salutations. Good night'

Mama told Papa of Miss Mary-Rose's intention to teach me after school until 4 o'clock every day.

'That teacher can do what she wants with Atarhe as she likes. I am tired of the woman's disturbance.' Mama did not say anything. I took Papa's answer to be a yes.

School was the usual way that Tuesday. In the morning, Miss Mary-Rose asked us to recite the alphabets and numbers 1 to 100. She also asked us to recite the multiplication table from the table of two to twelve. It was a lot of fun. She was a teacher to enjoy and love.

'Boys and girls,' she called out.

'Yes, aunty'

'Children, children,' she called again.

'Yes aunty,' the thunderous response went again.

'Sit down and clap for yourselves,' she said. The class shook with a loud applause.

'Very good,' she said, smiling, 'Now, we are going to have a little fun today because school is all about having fun as you learn'

'Okay, Aunty'

'Let's play What I Want To Be,' she said, writing the words on the board.

'What is our game?'

'What I want to be,' we chorused.

'Very good'

'Now, who wants to be a lawyer?' she asked. Most of the girls and a few boys raised their hands saying 'Aunty, I'

'Aunty, me'

'Very good. Now let's sing for them. You know the song, standard living, standard living,' she started the song as the prospective lawyers stood on their feet. The class went on singing '*Sandalili, sandalili,*' fixing the professions in the required part of the song.

'Wonderful children. How many people want to be doctors?' she asked. This time the boys were more than the girls. We sang the song again. She called up to ten professions with some pupils raising their hands over two to three times for what they wanted to be. Amidst all these, I did not raise my hand. I did not want to be anything.

'Atarhe,' Miss Mary-Rose called, 'Why don't you stand up and tell the class what you want to be '

I stood up. 'I don't know what I want to be, aunty,' I said.

'Oh'

'Aunty, she is NFA. She does not know what she wants. No future ambition,' Gift laughed out.

'Keep quiet.' 'Aunty shouted back at Gift, don't say bad things about other people. Is that clear? Class, is that clear?'

'Yes, aunty' the class chorused.

'Atarhe, tell us the things that you like doing'

'I like reading storybooks and I like to write what I learn out of them. I also like writing down anything I like'

'Good. So you'd like to be like those people that write storybooks. They are called writers?' 'enh.'

I did not answer.

'Well class, clap for Atarhe.' The class gave a roaring applause for me. I stood wondering why she asked them to clap for me.

'Class, Atarhe likes to write and she would like to be a writer. She wants to be like those people who write your storybook. Is it not true, Atarhe?'

'Yes, aunty,' I stuttered. I did not know if I wanted to be a writer or something else. I just said yes. I was sure Miss Mary-Rose wanted to cover up for me to prevent the class from laughing at me. 'So, who wants to be a writer like Atarhe?' A few students raised their hands and we sang the song one more time.

'Okay, children. Did we have fun?' she asked.

'Yes, aunty'

'That's good. So we should all work hard to be what we want to be. Is that okay?'

'Yes, aunty'

The bell for break went.

'Let's go and buy biscuit,' Dami suggested.

'Okay'.

'So, do you really like writing like aunty said?' Dami asked, after we had bought the biscuits.

'This biscuit is sweet, *shey?* I asked.

'Tarhe answer me, *na*. Do you like to write?' he asked again. I looked at him like I did not hear the question.

'Tarhe, *na,*' He pressed on.

'I don't know Dami. I don't know what I even like. Aunty just said that I want to write so that the class will not call me NFA again'

'Dami, how many years are you?' I asked.

'I am eight years old. My birthday is on the 20th of December,' He said.

'Five days before Christmas day and four days before Christmas watchinight,' I said, smiling. I chewed the biscuits as I put them in my mouth, one after the other.

'You are senior to me,' Dami said.

I nodded. 'What do you want to be?' I asked.

'You did not see when I raised my hand when Aunty said Engineers?' he asked.

'Okay, that is true'. I did not ask him why he wanted to be an Engineer. I just pictured him wearing thick hats and big black boots to work. I ate my biscuits and threw the wrap on the floor. The bell rang. I met Miss Mary-Rose after school as planned. She did not teach me on that first day. She asked me a lot of questions on my life at home, things I liked and disliked, things that made me happy and sad. She was writing some things down in her blue jotter. We spoke on and on and I went home after school. She gave me money to board a motorcycle. My day's letter which I wrote when I got home was about all we had discussed.

7

Evening classes with Miss Mary-Rose was something I looked forward to every day. I started working on the letters of the alphabet. She asked me to write them every day. I started knowing the difference between the letters b and d. Each day she gave me series of compositions to write. This evening, she asked me to write a composition on my family. I went home and wrote the composition with better spellings. I did the rest of my homework and wrote my letter.

Dear lettar,

Aunty Mary-Rose has been very good to me. she tought me how to spell her name well. She made me to understand things bettar. She has explained the difference b/w b and d and now I can write them bettar. You would notice that I have not been mis spelling words that have d with b again. I am very happy that she is my teachar. She is my best teachar. I will write her a composition. I will call it My Best Teachar. She will like it, abi? Yes, I think you agree with me. thank you so much for you are a good friend. You are the only one that have been with me since all these days. I love you, lettar. Thank you for

being there to talk to when I had nobody to understanb me. I am
happy to be your friend. Thank you. thank you, lettar.

Your friend,
Atarhe

I wrote the composition as a surprise for her. I put the paper in my bag and went out to play with Johwo. I was happy. I was a ten year old happy girl. I was sure this term was going to be better, better than the rest I have had that left a bitter taste like that of bile in my mouth.

The next day at school, I told Aunty that I had a surprise composition for her in addition to the one she asked me to write. She asked that I put both on her table. I put the surprise composition inside my afternoon class notebook and kept it on her desk. She must have read them both when we went out for break. Break was fun. I joined Johwo for our food and I watched as Dami went to play ball. I prayed Miss Mary-Rose liked the composition. I was happy when the bell that signalled the end of school for the day went and I said my goodbyes to Johwo and Dami and also to Chinyere afterwards, I sat down waiting for her to come and give me my evening lessons. She held the paper I had written my composition on in her right hand. I waited anxiously for her to say something about it. She finally spoke up.

'Atarhe, do you always write this?' she asked.
'No, aunty. I wrote it specially for you,' I said.
'But it is not addressed to me,' she said.

'Aunty, see na, I wrote My best teacher. Are you not seeing it?' I asked.

'Then, you must have given me the wrong paper,' she said, 'This is your letter'

'Oh. Aunty, sorry. I will bring your composition tomorrow,' I said.

'Okay. Here is your letter.' She handed the letter to me. No one had ever seen my letters before. She was the first. I wondered what she thought about it. She taught me some topics on Elementary Science. Before we went out of school, she asked me what the letters were about.

'I just write them,' I said.

'Why? Do you find confidence in them?' she asked.

'I don't know, aunty but whenever I write them, I feel safe and free,' I said.

'That was a good choice to make. How many have you written?' she asked.

'I don't know how many but there are several of them. I have been writing them for some time now.'

'Can I see them? I want to read them,' she said.

'Okay. I will bring them for you tomorrow,' I said.

'Thank you'

She gave me *okada* fare and I went home. I kept thinking why she wants my letter. Those letters were important to me and I had never thought of showing them to anybody. But it was Miss Mary-Rose. I could trust her with my letters. The first thing I did on getting home was going under my bed to get the letters from the bucket I kept them. I drew the bucket from its position and poured out the folded sheets of paper on the bed. I started arranging them one after the other. I did not hear Johwo come in. She had come to call me for my food.

'Mama is calling you. She said you should come and eat,' she said, 'What are those papers?' she asked.

'Nothing,' I said.

'Ehen,' she said. Her eyes were full of suspicion. She came to the bed and hurriedly picked two of the letters and ran off. She took them to Mama who was in the parlour. She was reading a copy of *Daily Strength Devotional.*

'Mama, Johwo have been writing plenty letters. See them.' She handed the letters to Mama. Mama opened the first one. She read through it. She read the other one. I had stayed back in the room. I put the rest of the letters in my bag. I heard Mama call my name.

'Yes, Mama,' I answered, from my room.

'*Mo,* come and tell me what you are writing,' she said. Her voice was casual. She did not sound angry. I knew she was not going to shout at me for any reason.

'I am coming, Mama'

She was in the parlour. Johwo stood by her. I did not know Johwo wanted to tell Mama about my letters. I wondered what she wanted Mama to do with the letters or what she thought they were all about.

'Johwo, go and do your homework,' Mama said.

'Papa will not tell me to go o. It is only you that will be telling me this one,' she said, grumbling.

'Will you leave this place,' Mama said, picking up her slippers off her right foot and threatening to throw it at

Johwo. Johwo mumbled a few words about Mama always being in my favour and left the parlour.

'Silly girl,' Mama said behind her, 'Tarhe, sit down'

I sat down. The chair sank in. I sank in with it.

'What are all these letters about, my daughter? I mean, since when have you been writing them?' she asked

'I.. Mama, it has been a little time. Not too long,' I answered.

'My child, why did you not tell me?' she asked.

'Mama, I did not tell anybody about my letters because they help me to forget all what people use to say about me. The letters give me the chance to understand myself. I never knew that anybody will see them, Mama.' I explained that Miss Mary-Rose saw the letter instead of the composition and how she had asked for the rest of the letters.

'My daughter, I am very sorry. I did not know that you were going through all of these things alone,' she said. She drew closer to me on the chair and embraced me. 'It is well.' I smiled at her. She went to the room with me and asked Johwo not to mention the letters to Papa. Johwo was sure to do otherwise. When she was bent on something there was no turning back. That evening Papa came home and Johwo welcomed him with her already memorised report on my letters. Papa was about to eat his food when she told him.

'What letters?' he asked, washing his hands to eat his meal of *eba* and *banga* soup.

'Papa, I don't even know o. I saw her arranging the papers in her bag,' she said.

'Atarhe, can be very funny sometimes,' Papa said, laughing. 'Johwo, leave me let me eat my food, *jare*'

Papa did not talk about my letters again. Papa took me lightly. Every issue concerning me was not worth talking about. I did not have a say in Papa's life. What I said or did, did not matter to him. I am even sure that if someone should be seeking for a child, Papa could easily give me out to the individual. He settled down to battle a piece of *kpomo* in the soup. He closed his eyes and winced as his incisors bit into the hard cooked piece of leather material. I went to bed early that night. I did not want to have a long and inquisitive talk with Johwo, asking me questions that I had no answers to or the ones I had answers that I could not reveal to her. I did not write my letter that night. I dreamed that Miss Mary-Rose collected my letters and tore them all into pieces and laughing like those witches showed in Nigerian movies that we watched on TV. I woke up. It was 4 o'clock in the morning. Johwo was sleeping soundly. I stood up and walked on tip-toed to the reading table. I wrote one more letter. I was not giving that to Miss Mary-Rose. I was going to keep the letter for myself.

Dear lettar,

Do you know that aunty Mary-rose has seen the other lettars that I have been writing to you all this time. I do not know what she wants to do with them but she ask that I bring the other ones that I write to you. I will not give her this one that I am writing to you now. I will keep this one. I will give her the rest of them. Do you know that Johwo even went to tell Mama about the lettars when she saw me

arranging them but Mama did not answer her. She na went to tell
Papa that I was writing lettars. She does not even understand what
my lettars are about. She just does not know. She talks and talks. I
don't really blame her sef. She is just tinking that Mama use to
support me too much. I don't really blame her. I use to feel the same
way with she and Papa. I don't really think that Mama use to favour
me. Mama like both of us in the same way. I just know that. Let's
wait and see what aunty Mary-Rose want to do with it.

Your friend,
Atarhe

I did not feel sleep in my eyes anymore but I lay on my bed
all the same. Johwo stirred and rolled over and placed her
right leg on mine. I smiled. I gently brushed off her leg and
closed my eyes to let sleep in.

It was a school day again. I went with the letters to
school. Classes went on smoothly. Dami and I went out
for break together. I told him about the letters. I told him
the reasons why I started writing the letters. I finally told
him about my sour relationship with my father. Dami is a
good ear to talk to, understanding and different from people
I have encountered. He was as safe as my letters. School
was over for the day and we were informed that some
inspectors were coming over on Monday to inspect the
school. We were asked to dress up in our best. The rest of
the pupils started trooping out of the school to their various
destinations. I stayed back with Miss Mary-Rose. I gave
her the letters. She bound them together with a rubber band

from her drawer and kept them in her handbag. She taught me spellings with the use of dictations. She also showed me the use of punctuation marks. We treated the Full stops, Comma and Apostrophe. She told me to be cautious of the Apostrophe. I learnt a lot that evening.

The mid-term break was drawing close. It was the week after. I wondered if I was still going to have lessons with Miss Mary-Rose. The next day being a Saturday, we went to the farm a few hours before noon and branched at Mama's shop afterwards. I kept on practicing on my handwriting in the new writing note that Miss Mary-Rose had bought for me. Mama was happy that I was learning faster. I was happy. I hoped Papa was happy as well. My Catechism class was going on smoothly. We were to write tests soon. If I did well, I would be qualified to be amongst those who would receive the sacrament of the Holy Eucharist at the same time as Johwo. Mama was very helpful all the way. She taught me more on Catechism and we studied every day in the evening together with Johwo.

On Monday, after the inspection, Miss Mary-Rose told me that she could not return my letters that day. She said they were with her uncle. She said he liked them and wanted to see them and know what he could make of them. She said something about him being the editor of Reality Press. She said Reality Press was a publishing house for real life stories. That was when I knew Aunty lives in her uncle's house with him alongside his family. His two children were twin boys attending one of the Catholic boys secondary school in Benin city. Miss Mary-Rose had studied English and Literary studies and she had plans of editing in her uncle's publishing house where he works after her one year service. She said that he might want to work on my letters either for an article or as a book. I did not want anyone keeping my letters. I said okay to it all the same. She promised to return the letters to me on Thursday before Mid-term break which would commence from Friday through the next Monday. We were having Catechism test on the Monday which was the second and last day of the break. I had to prepare for it. I told Mama that Miss Mary-Rose had my best interest at heart and that she assured me that my letters were in safe hands and would be returned to me in time soon.

'You should not worry about this. Let's think about your test on Monday. I know you will write well through our lord Jesus Christ. Amen'

'Amen,' I said.

On Thursday, Miss Mary-Rose told me her uncle was still going through the letters and had not reached a decision and so I could not get the letters. I was getting worried. I did not know what my letters were going through. Why was her Uncle keeping them? I wanted my letters back.

'Aunty, when will he na give me?' I asked.

'Soon, my dear,' she answered. Soon could be a day or a week or even more. I wanted my letters back to me, back to the broken blue bucket, back to under my bed where they belonged.

The mid-term break on Friday got a lot of pupils in jubilation. They ran off saying how well they were going to enjoy the holidays. I walked with Dami. Chinyere had gone off with her friends. Dami and I went to call Johwo and we walked together. Dami left us when we got to the junction which led to Dami's street. We walked on until we got home. I ate with Johwo. Mama made us yam porridge, this time with beans. I did not like beans so much. I usually ate mostly yam. I was still in wonder of what might become of my letters. Miss Mary-Rose was not being clear with what was happening with my letters. I wanted them back. They were mine. I missed them. I started my mid-term break with writing another letter that evening.

Dear lettar,

Aunty Mary-rose have not still return my lettars til today. I want my lettars back. She is saying her uncle is reading them. She is saying he want to use them for something. I don't know what ~~trhey~~ they are doing with them. Aunty shuold just give them back to me. you know how me I like all the whole lettars. Do you think that her uncle will use the lettars for something good? I don't know. Ehm, I should just calm down and like Mama said they will give me back and aunty is a good person. Mid-term break have start. I will not na see Dami for that time. I have catchism test on Monday. Pray for me to pass. Mama said that I will pass and I believe. I will then be receiving communion. Papa will be happy. That time I will not be a shame to him. I will not be a dullarb. I will be his daughtar that he have always want. I am smiling. I know you are smiling too.. your lettars will soon come.

> *Your friend,*
> *Atarhe*

Mid-term break was the way I expected it to be. We helped Mama in the farm and shop. We went for Friday evening Mass and Saturday morning Mass. On Saturday there was infant baptism. Papa was one of the babies' Godfather. The baby's name was Stephen. His mother is a friend of Mama. Papa stood behind the mother carrying the child in his navy blue cassock-like dress. There were three other babies to be baptised making a total of four. Some prayers and vows were said and taken, and the babies baptised in the baptismal font with Father Sixtus pouring water over their heads and saying the child's name with the words 'I baptise you in the name of the father and of the son and of the holy spirit. Amen.' And finally he placed a white cloth on the child's head.

'Mama as Stephen is now Papa's Godson, is he our God brother?' I asked, pronouncing Stephen as step hen as I have always pronounced.

'Stephen, not step hen and there is no word like God brother, my child,' she said, laughing lightly.

'Ok, Mama,' I laughed also. 'I would be a baby's Godmother too,' I said.

'Yes. You will,' Mama said. 'Even Johwo too,' she added.

Monday Catechism test was taken by the Catechism teacher, Mr Ariavwote, who had set our questions for us. There were two stages: the paper test and the oral test. The paper came first with ten questions and then the orals. The questions for the orals were from our Catechism book. Mr Ariavwote asked us the questions randomly. I had done well in the orals. I prayed that I also did well in the written test. The results were to be given to us the next day. I prayed silently to pass this first test. It would show that I was ready for the sacrament. Papa did not fail to ask us how well the test went after evening Mass which was usually after catechism class on Monday. Mama did not come. Papa mentioned her not feeling too well. Johwo did not take time in saying that she had done well. She was full of confidence. He said that his only prayer was for us both to pass the catechism and receive the sacrament. For that minute, Papa did not sound hostile to me. He was calm and sounded like the father I always wanted. I found my lips forming into a smile. Papa took notice of it.

'Why are you smiling, Tarhe?' he asked.

'Nothing o, Papa. I just remember something,' I said.

'You are always up to something,' he scoffed.

All three of us got on the *okada* and Papa drove us home. We stopped to buy bread at one of those kiosks in our street for dinner. I made a hot cup of bournvita and drank with a slice of bread I had cut out from the loaf. I spread some butter on it and ate dipping the bread in my tea. I enjoyed it better that way. I went to bed happy that night. I dreamed that Papa had come to my room and asked me what my letters were about. I told him I wrote that I wanted him to love me like he loved Johwo. He took my hand and told me that he loved me and was happy to have me as his first child and daughter. Then, he stepped out of my room into the town. I called out to him to stay but he faded into thin air and I never saw him again. I woke up. It was 6.00am. Johwo was still fast asleep. I sat on the bed pondering on the dream when Mama came in with a lantern in her right hand. There was no power supply. Seeing me already awake, she asked me to go to the parlour for morning prayers. She woke Johwo up. Johwo stirred and mumbled a few words, stood up and made way through the back door from the corridor to the toilet to ease herself. Mama waited for her while I went on ahead. They both came in and we started the prayers. I had mixed feelings about resuming school that morning. The mid-term break was over. I wanted to go to school but I also wanted to stay back from the heat of the environment. Johwo wore a new hairstyle which she made on the Saturday before. Her hair was made into beautiful and neat all back plaits with no parting. The hairstyle exposed Johwo's protruding forehead which we teased her with as *ogo* which meant bottle. Perhaps, it was a bit too tight. Johwo had to make the hair at a hair maker's place as Mama did not have the strength to make the hair. Mama had given her money and I accompanied her to the lady's place. The people call her Mama Paulina or Madam salon. She was good at her job. The hair came out beautifully well but I think Johwo must have been too used to Mama's hands that this one was a little too tight for her unlike Mama's. Although Johwo did not complain, I knew it was tight. After prayers, we took our bath and came back to meal of beans and dodo. Mama gave us money for snacks during break. I hurriedly combed my hair which was growing out again. I wanted Miss Mary-Rose to compliment me that I looked nice and return my letters. I asked her about the letters immediately after assembly.

106

'Aunty, have your uncle given you my letters?' I asked.

'My dear, no. Okay, I promise I will bring them tomorrow,' she said.

That was not the pleasant answer I wanted to hear but all the same I nodded to show my approval. Dami did not come to school that day. Chinyere had said that she did not know why he had not come. I did not talk to any of Dami's other friends and so I could not ask anyone. I thought of going to visit him but I did not know his house although I knew the street.

'We would ask him when he comes to school tomorrow,' I said to Chinyere.

The next day, Dami came to school. He said he was sick during the mid-term break and so he could not come the day before.

'Sorry,' I said the words as though I had offended him and was seeking forgiveness.

'Thank you. Have aunty given you your letters?' he asked.

I shook my head. 'She said today, *sha,*' I said.

'Okay. Have you written more?' he asked.

I nodded. 'I use to write them every day,' I said.

'Will I read?' he asked.

'Let aunty give me this one first,' I said. That was the answer that came to mind. I did not give a yes or no as an answer. I was not sure I wanted anyone else to read those letters. During our evening class that day, Miss Mary-Rose told me that her uncle would like to see me in person.

'Aunty, me?' I asked.

'Yes, Atarhe. See, I think he likes your letters. I have read them too. We could tell a story with it. Won't you like that?' she asked.

'Aunty, I don't know. Let me tell Mama first.'

'I will come and see your Mama with you today after lesson. Is that okay?'

'Okay, aunty'

We studied topics in Mathematics. The second test was coming soon and then the promotion examinations. She was bound on making me pass unlike getting the same failure like in the past.

8

Miss Mary-Rose had told Mama about her uncle's intention of meeting me in person when we both went home that evening. Mama told her that she had no idea of books and their business but if her uncle was interested in meeting me, she had no objection. Miss Mary-Rose went further to ask if she could take me to her Uncle's place by the weekend. Mama told her that she would discuss it with Papa and would keep her informed. When Papa was told about the proposed meeting with Miss Mary-Rose's uncle, he said that I could go as long as that woman did not put him in trouble. Those were his very own words, 'that woman.' On Friday, Catechism test results were announced. I had scored 9 out of 10 in the orals and 6 out of 10 in the written test. In total, I scored 15 out of 20. The pass mark was 14 and I was happy. Johwo scored 18. Papa was happy. Mama was happy. Johwo was happy. I was the happiest.

That Saturday morning when Miss Mary-Rose came to pick me up, we just had breakfast. I wore my purple gown that had the picture of Cinderella, the purple colour fading out to a dull lilac. I combed my hair and waited for her in the parlour when she came. She dressed up smartly in a yellow pair of skinny jeans and a sleeveless black chiffon top. She held a small black purse with LV designs on it. I presumed she wore skirts only on school days to work. All the time, I had seen her outside school, she wore trousers. She greeted Mama and Papa and also said hello to Johwo. She told Papa and Mama that we had to leave early so that she would bring me back home on time. Her uncle, Mr Alfred Avwenaughe, lived in Lori Estate in Ughelli. His house was a beautiful structure. A beautiful huge black gate with gold markings led into the interlocked compound. There were a number of flower pots holding beautiful flowers like the Christmas tree, the Aloe vera and one that looked like palm leaves. There were three cars in the compound—a Mercedes jeep and two others, also of Mercedes brand. The house was a brown and cream painted bungalow and we walked through the main door into the house.

'Tarhe, sit down. Let me call uncle,' she said.

'Okay, aunty.' She went through the door leading to the passage. I looked round the living room. It was beautiful. The brown coated chairs matched beautifully with the curtains and blinds. There was an air conditioner at the end of the room before the vault that separated the parlour from the dining table. It was not on though. She came back soon with a cold bottle of Fanta in her right hand and a cork opener and straw in her left.

Atarhe, uncle will soon be here. You'd like some drink, I'm sure,' she said, opening the drink. The cork fell on the

110

tiled floor making a clinking sound. She picked it up and placed on the stool which she had placed in front of me.

'Thank you, aunty.' I took sips through the pink straw which she had placed in the bottle of drink.

'See your orange tongue,' Miss Mary-Rose laughed.

I smiled. Her uncle walked in. He was a tall man, dark-skinned and had a pair of glasses on.

'Ah, Ah. The young, inspirational Atarhe,' he said.

'Miguo, sir,' I greeted in Urhobo.

'Vrendo, my daughter. Are you enjoying your drink?' he asked, full of smiles.

'Yes, sir,' I did not smile back at him. I suddenly felt suffocated in the airy room. I kept sipping the drink.

'That's good,' he said.

There was a brief silence.

'How did you think about writing those beautiful letters of yours?' he asked.

I placed the bottle containing about three-quarter of the Orange-coloured drink.

'Sir, I just started to write the letters. Is not as if I write them for anybody to see. Papa and people around me just start to see me that I yam without brain. I did not born myself like this so I don't know why they use to do me like this.' I paused. 'But uncle, I yam not an imbecile like they are saying. Since nobody na use to listen to me, I started to write the letters'

'Wow. That's very thoughtful of you,' he said. He turned to Miss Mary-Rose. 'Rose, you were right about this girl'

'I told you, uncle'

'Atarhe, did your aunty here tell you about Reality Press?' he asked.

I nodded. 'Yes, she said that that is the place that you use to work,' I said.

'You are right. I am the Editor of the press. My work is to go through the books presented to us and see if we would publish them'

'Okay, sir. But, where is the place?' I asked.

'It's in Warri, my dear, not in Ughelli,' he replied.

'I want to publish your letters as a collection of your thoughts and we will write more on them. Would you not like that?' he asked.

I said nothing. He had placed his glasses on the stool beside him. I stared at them.

'Tarhe, to publish your letters is turning them to one book like your storybooks. Your aunty said you liked storybooks,' he said.

'Won't you like that?' Miss Mary-Rose added.

I lifted my eyes from the glasses and said, 'I don't know, Aunty'

'Why?'

'I don't know if I want people to be reading my letters,' I said.

Miss Mary-Rose smiled. 'Uncle, let me explain to her better,' she said.

'Okay. Atarhe, finish your drink. I would be in my room.' He went back through the passage door which Miss Mary-Rose had earlier passed to his room. She then went on to lecture me on book publishing process and that the message that I wanted to send through those letters would be heard. She said I would not have to keep the thoughts in my head again, suffering and craving for peace of mind. She also told me I would be paid some amount of money which she called royalty. She told me that Reality Press would help me to become better. I told her that if Mama and Papa agreed to it, then she and her uncle had my full support. She took the empty bottle back inside and told her uncle that she was taking me home. Her uncle gave her a thousand naira, in the five hundred naira denomination. I said thank you and we left. We boarded an *okada* and went back to my place. She told Mama about her uncle's proposal to have my letters published by his publishing house. She explained the basics of publishing the letters to Mama. As expected, Mama said that we had to wait for Papa's approval. Mama did not forget to tell Papa about it when he came home. Papa said that he sent me to be a pupil in school and not to become a second daughter to a youth corper who had no sense of respect for him. He said I was not asked to write letters that people wanted to market on. Mama tried explaining to him but he told her to stop supporting uncalled for extra-curricular activities in his home. I was silent all through. Mama told me that we would visit Father Sixtus and tell him about the situation.

'Your father listens to Fada,' she said, 'He would talk to him for us,' Mama said.

On Sunday evening, Mama told Papa that we were going to see Father Sixtus. He agreed to it and did not ask why. When we got to the parish house, Father was upstairs in his room. Father Sixtus' room was more of a self-contain. It had a parlour, bathroom and then his room where he slept. We knocked on the door and entered waiting for him in the parlour. When he came out, he greeted us and said asked that we go to the balcony as there was no light and that the room was hot.

'Mrs Onanefe,' he said, 'What brings you to our small place?' he asked, smiling.

Mama laughed. 'Fada, it is a small issue. I wanted to come with Atarhe, that's why I did not come on the days of your office,' she explained.

'No, problem, Madam,' he said.

He gave me his Ipad after opening the Talking Tom app for me. He gave me a demo of how to play the game and I went inside the room to play. Mama talked with him for long before she called out to me.

'Atarhe'

'Yes, Mama.' I went out to meet them.

Father Sixtus asked me to sit by him. He smiled at me.

'My smallie, Mama has told me everything. You want me to talk to your Papa, is that not so?'

'Yes, Fada. I want Papa to agree. I want the message in those letters to speak out,' I said

He smiled again. 'You would have your will, my daughter. Keep praying to the blessed Virgin. She would support you,' he assured me.

'Yes, Fada'

'Thank you so much, Fada. We should be going,' Mama said.

'Okay, Madam. Let us pray'

Father Sixtus led us in the prayers.

'Before I forget,' he said, after the prayers. He went inside the room. I watched his gait closely as he walked fast through the door. Mama and I followed him and sat in the parlour. He came back with a white nylon bag. There was a packet of *Mcvities* digestive biscuit in it. He handed it over to me.

'That's for you and Johwo for passing your Catechism test,' he said.

I smiled showing a full set of teeth. 'Miguo, Fada,' I said.

'Thank you, fada,' Mama said.

'You are welcome. Greet catechist for me. I will see him after Mass tomorrow,' he said.

'We will,' Mama answered.

Johwo was happy to receive the biscuits. We ate them with cups of bournvita that evening. We went to bed early that night as there was school the next day. Johwo had told me that she was sorry for trying to get my letters seized when she reported to Papa. She asked what the letters were about and I told her. She said she would like them to be published. I smiled. I told her to sit down with me while I wrote the one for the night.

Dear lettar,

I brought someone for you today. It's my sistar. The one I use to tell you about. she is now in support of me talking to you. lettar, I don't

115

know how long I will keep talking to you. they said they want keep all of you that I have written inside a book. Like those my storybook I use to read. Lettar, I don't want you to go.but you know that I would always want the best for all of us. I should let them publish the lettars. It would be good for all of us. Good night. Johwo is saying good night too.

> *Your friend,*
> *Atarhe*

I woke up with tired eyes the next morning. The night was short and cold. It had rained. We had a very hot bath, as we usual normal quantity of cold water. We wore the sweaters Papa had bought for us during his trip to Onitsha with his friend a year ago. I enjoyed the classes for the rest of the day. They were interesting. We did two pages of quantitative aptitude workbook. I had scored 7 out of 12 questions. I was getting better. Gradually, the feeling of being a worthy student crept in. I had prayed this morning for Papa to listen to Father Sixtus in the evening. Miss Mary-Rose announced that the Friday after this one, the midterm continuous assessment test would commence. She asked us to prepare for it. Dami and I went out for break together. Beatrice, that same girl who had troubled me some time ago in class came to meet us under the mango tree. This time, she was with Gift, her friend.

'Atarhe,' she said.

'Yes?'

'Test is coming o, you will not go and read. Be sitting down here and be doing friend with him,' she said.

'Is it your business?' I asked. The words flew out. I was surprised that I was able to answer her that way. Dami did not say anything.

'Ehen? So that's what he has been teaching you. To talk anyhow to people who even when they add ten of your brain it's not up to their own,' Gift said.

'What is your own?' Dami asked, standing up. 'Una dey crase?' he asked again, in pidgin.

'It's you that is crazy,' Beatrice said.

Dami picked up a stick and hit her with it. Gift ran towards me, pulling at my ears and pinching me. I did not fight back. I did not know how to fight. Moreover, Mama said never to fight back, so I didn't fight. Aunty Rachel came and stopped the fight she asked us to go her class, primary 6A, and kneel down with our eyes closed and hands up. We kept the painful position for the rest of break she afterwards came and cautioned us after each our of us gave our own side of the story. On my return to class, I told Dami he should have never started the fight with her because she was not worth the punishment.

'I did not get punished because of her. I did it for you. You are my friend and I would not let anybody talk to you the way they like,' he said.

I smiled. 'Thank you, Dami,' I said 'You are a good friend'

'Are you preparing for test?' he asked.

'Yes, aunty has been teaching me very well,' I answered. 'Things have become clearer since she started teaching me.'

'That is a good thing,' he said.

'What of you, *shey* you are preparing well?' I asked.

'Very good'

During evening lessons that day with Miss Mary-Rose, she asked if Papa had agreed to the publication of the letters. I told her about Father Sixtus plan to talk to him after Mass that evening. She taught me till 4.00pm and I left her in school because she said she was staying till six. Mama asked me to prepare *eba* for myself. I made the *eba* while Mama heated up the beans soup made the night before. She served the soup hot. I sat down to eat. Johwo was plaiting the hair of her doll. The left arm of the doll was off. I watched her part the hair and make it into single braids as I chewed my lumps of *eba* ensuring to pick pieces of dried fish along with the soup. We went for Mass that evening. Papa met with Father Sixtus after Mass. We went to the parish house with them as Father wanted to have a long talk with him. Father Sixtus talked to Papa trying to convince him that having the letters published as a collection was for the benefit of all, most especially me. Papa argued saying that those things were a distraction.

'Fada, you know how Tarhe is with book work. I don't want all these distractions. She is already physically challenged. This one is a problem, Fada,' he said.

'Catechist, that's what I am saying. This will stop all her crudity, her fear and the insecurity that she feels. Catechist, I want you to appreciate your daughter. Appreciate her every being. This girl did not just become Atarhe by her will, it is by God,' Father said.

After much talking, Papa reluctantly consented to it. I was very happy. Papa's yes was the only hurdle to having those letters published. Miss Mary-Rose was happy to hear it when I told her the day after and she promised to share the good news with her uncle. I felt this inner peace, this fulfilment. I felt love for the first time. I was in love with having to create this book, the chance to make a decision. Being the imbecile they called me had proved to be a blessing. Mama always said that every disappointment always turns out to be a blessing. Now, I see that a good mother's words never lie. I closed my eyes. I could breathe freely. I did not suffocated in my own skin. I felt beautiful and blessed. I felt like my father's daughter.

The next day, I was told that I was getting published. My work had being accepted and they needed the rest of my letters. An agreement had been signed. Mr Alfred had insisted on having me run through series of test on my mental condition to know my IQ and the condition of my brain and how well I could heal or manage my condition, whatever and however it was. I did not know how well to thank God for bringing Miss Mary-Rose into my life and to thank her for being the instrument in God's hand. Papa said he had no money to run tests on me, and that he felt there was no need Mr Alfred told him he was footing the bills. Papa was grateful. He said whatever test that needed to be carried out should be done before my next C.A test commenced. It was agreed that the next Saturday, they would go with me to Warri for the test. The publishing house was our first point of call on that Saturday. It was another Saturday with Mr Alfred and Miss Mary-Rose. This time, his wife came with us. She apologised for not being around the last time I came to her home. She had been out to visit a friend. She was pleased to meet me. She was a very nice woman, like Mama. She was about the same height as Mama and she spoke Urhobo as if she was eating boiled yam with palm oil. She was dark in complexion like her husband and had a space between her upper incisors when she talked. She was beautiful.

Reality Press was an accommodating place. It was an excursion for me. I said yes to virtually everything that he said, that I was asked. I was given a free copy of Alfred Avwenaughe's *The Road I walked*. It was an auto-biography on his life and how he grew to success. We left there for St. Anthony Hospital. As we drove past the Effurun roundabout, I rolled down the window and looked at the huge structure that was being built there. We arrived at the hospital. I saw goose pimples form on the surface of my skin. I hated hospitals. They smelt of drugs and sick people. I was afraid of needles and knowing that as I was going to have a test, I feared the more. I was nervous and uneasy. Miss Mary-Rose noticed and asked me to relax and that the test would not be painful. The Doctor soon came and asked for us to see him in the consulting room. He asked me a few questions which I answered and then, he asked Miss Mary-Rose some questions.

'Who are you to her?' he asked her.

'I'm her class teacher,' she answered.

'That's good. I would want you to answer some questions'

'Okay, sir'

'How active is she in class?' he asked. Miss Mary-Rose told him about my performance in class from the time she started work as my class teacher. He went on to ask for other symptoms. He asked if I was day-dreamy, easily confused, mentally foggy and if I stared frequently. Miss Mary-Rose answered the questions to the best of her knowledge.

'This might be a case of SCT,' he said.

'And what might that be?' Mr Alfred asked.

'Sluggish cognitive tempo. It is a condition found in children to have them mentally slow, not sociable and very timid. She has most of the symptoms. She is mentally foggy, usually afraid, easily confused and she stares a lot like she is doing now,' he said. I did not realise that I was staring at the wall. I turned to face the Doctor when Mrs Avwenaughe poked me.

'So, what can we do Doctor? We will run a few tests first, then we will know for sure'

'Okay, Doc,' Mr Alfred said.

We were led to the room where the MRI machine was. I was scared when I was told that I would go inside it to be scanned. Miss Mary-Rose assured me that I would be fine. I changed to the hospital's green gown and was strapped into the machine. I closed my eyes in fear. After the scan, I ran to hug Miss Mary-Rose. I wanted her to hold me tight. I was scared.

'It's alright, my dear,' she said, patting my back. The results were studied and the doctors talked with Mr Alfred and his wife. I stayed outside with Miss Mary-Rose. They came out soon. Mrs Avwenaughe went to the cashier to pay the bills and Mr Alfred told me that he would come back the week after to take my drugs. He had a booklet in his hand which he was to give to my parents on managing cases of SCT. We drove back home to Ughelli. I had no idea what it all meant but I was happy that I had good people by my side all the way. I looked out of the rolled up window, watching the pedestrians as they walked on the sides of the road. I soon fell asleep.

9

Mama coddled me a lot after the SCT test. I had a series of dreams where I found myself in the MRI machine. I found myself spinning and spinning, till and I woke up either in the night or morning. It went on for about three days before the dreams stopped. Johwo and I were preparing hard for the up-coming test. We read together. Perhaps, Johwo wanted to be supportive of me. Papa's attitude also changed a bit. My fear was curbed. It was no longer there. Miss Mary-Rose was the cocoon of a happy me. Our evening classes were smooth. I was being groomed to aim great grades this time in the test. I made sure I did not let anything distract me. I made sure not to be lethargic. I was enthusiastic about the test. I wanted to pass. I wanted to make everyone proud. From Mama, to Miss Mary-Rose, the Avwenaughe's, Johwo, Dami and most especially, Papa. I was living that dream. The dream in my letters. I owed those letters everything. The strength that crept into me was unexpected. I was no longer that weak Atarhe with no future ambition, I was Atarhe the transformed girl. Mr Alfred had gotten my drugs from the hospital. Mama had rained blessings on him so much that if the blessings were water, he would go home drenched.

Dear lettar,

This your friend is living a great life. I am very happy. So happy that I can't thank you enough for all your help. You were my friend the time I needed someone to talk to. Mr Alfred, aunty Mary-rose uncle has been helping us. He has been taking care of us very much. He is a good man. I know that you like good people. Aunty Mary-rose and her uncle and even his wife are all good people. Mama have been praising him since. Ehen, do you know that even papa was happy. He have not been shouting at me since they did that test. You know that I have been having plenty dreams since that test inside that machine. It was very scarding to be inside that thing but now it is fine. I use to swallow plenty mericine nowadays but is not bad. They say it will make me bettar. Lettar, this is what we have been praying for. Another test is coming and we must pass. I will pass. I am not afraid again. i yam a free girl. I am smiling and very happy. Even Fathar Sixtus was very happy when we told him. You know Fathar Sixtus na. Our Parish father. Everybody just happy. Thank you my friend.

Your Friend,
Atarhe

I told Dami about the MRI test I had in Warri while we were in school.

'Dami, I was afraid ehn, it was very scarding. I close my eyes tight ehn,' I narrated.

124

Dami laughed. 'Ehen, I can imagine. If I was there you would have not been afraid of the machine,' He said, holding my hand.

'I know,' I answered. Dami sounded like those Princes in Disney's stories who come to save the Princesses. I smiled at him. I was not sure if I wanted to but I felt the edges of my mouth crinkle in a weak smile. We read together for the rest of the break. I told him that I was happy that he was my friend and that he had been very good to me.

'Let's read. We will talk later,' he said.

We read till the end of break. Miss Mary-Rose had started test revision with the class. We attempted series of class works, assignments and also group works. At times, the groups were by seats or rows. She asked every pupil in class to say the problems they had in each subject that we offered. Each pupil stood up to talk while she asked the class monitor to write their thoughts down on a sheet of paper. I was expecting the test with full enthusiasm. I was not feeling any ounce of fear. Not for a minute. I was gradually crawling out of my shell. People became friendly with me. I was no longer called NFA. Everyone, especially the teachers, were surprised at my progressive performance in school.

Tuesday afternoon, Miss Mary-Rose apologised that we could not have evening class. This was because she had somewhere to be. I agreed and I went home with Johwo that evening.

'Atarhe, why are you home by this time?' Mama asked. She was sitting on an iron chair in front of the house by the veranda.

'Aunty Mary-Rose said that she is going somewhere today,' I answered.

'Okay, my child.' She turned to Johwo. 'My dear, how was school?' she asked, rubbing Johwo's chubby cheek softly with her right palm.

'Mama, it was fine. I am hungry o,' she said, rubbing her tummy and squeezing her lips to establish her point.

'Okay, let me go and serve your food before you rub that stomach out. I made jollof rice,' Mama said, getting up from the chair and brushing off the dirt from her black skirt with her hands.

'Yayy! Rice!' Johwo shouted. She ran into the house and she hit her leg on a stool.

Ouch, she groaned.

Mama shrilled. 'Johwo, be careful o, before you fall. I don't have that body to clean injury o. Did you hear?' she said the last three words in Urhobo.

'Yes, Mama,' she answered from within. 'Go and change your dress,' she said to me.

'Okay, Mama,' I said and went inside.

'Come and carry your food after you have removed your uniform,' Mama said to us as she walked through the corridor to the backyard where the kitchen was.

'Yes, Mama,' we answered. Johwo had already taken off the brown and green pinafore uniform which was our school uniform for girls. Boys wore shorts. She was in her petticoat made from china white material. She ran out of the room and went to carry her food from the kitchen. I laughed as she ran out. She must have been very hungry to

126

run out in that manner. I took off my own uniform and wore my blue jean shorts. I have had that shorts since I was seven and I was beginning to outgrown it. It already had a tear in one of the legs. I threw a pink shirt over my head and shoulders when I heard Mama's voice. She called out my name.

'I yam coming, Mama,' I said, in urhobo.

'The food will get cold. *Mo, o,*' she said.

She had served the rice in one of the stainless plates and plunged a star spoon into the heap of rice.

'You girls should eat and go and read for some time before your father comes,' Mama said.

'Mama, you did not put fish, o,' Johwo muttered.

'*Dooh*, I did not go out today. Tomorrow, there will be fish in your food, ehn,' Mama said.

'Oh, na,' Johwo grumbled on. Mama ignored her grumbling. We finished our food, washed it down our throats with cold water and went to get our books from the room to read. We sat on the veranda. There was no light and so it was too hot inside to read.

With the test drawing closer, Miss Mary-Rose revised a lot of topics with me. I understood a lot of things during the period of our lessons.

On the Friday of test, the papers were dropped on our tables and turned upside down as usual. The nervous feeling that I usually had during tests and examinations was not there anymore. I waited to turn the white A4 paper around and answer the questions printed in that same black font. There was a difference this time.

This time, I did not stare. This time, I was a girl who knew my problems and had developed the best means to overcome them. I prayed before the test and I started writing to the best of my knowledge. 'Pencils up!' I had not finished my work though but I had answered a lot of them. I did not want to get punished for late submission of my answer script. I submitted my paper and made the sign of the cross, wishing myself success in the test.

'Did you write well?' he voice asked. It sounded unfamiliar. I turned, it was Christabel, one of my classmates in school whom I had never talked to.

'I wrote well,' the words crawled out of my mouth.

Okay. Bye-bye, she said, waving her right hand at me.

'Bye-bye,' I said, saying the words almost in a whisper.

By Monday, as usual, the results would be out and then we would have the promotion exams to prepare for. When we got home, Mama was back from the shop to prepare food.

'My daughters have finished writing their test,' Mama said, turning the words into her own made music. 'How was it, my children?,' she asked.

'Mama, it was fine,' we answered.

'Thank God,' she said, raising her hands to words the ceiling in thanks. 'Before you say you are hungry, let me go and bring your food. There is beans in the pot. Will you eat it with *garri*?' she asked.

We answered positively. Beans and *garri* always tasted nice. Johwo usually ate hers with the *garri* soaked in water but I preferred having mine dry, stirring it together with the beans. We went for Catechism class later that evening. After class, before Mass one of the other catechumens walked up to me. I usually saw her in class but we never talked.

'Hi,' she said.

'Good evening,' I replied.

'How was your test in school?' she asked. I looked at her. She was not in my school. I was sure I had never seen her in Community Primary School before. I wondered how she knew we had written tests.

'Your sister said that you people wrote test today. *Shey*, you wrote well?' she asked.

'Yes, I wrote well. Very well. Thank you,' I said.

'Okay, Mass will soon start. Let us go inside,' she said.

'Okay. Ehn, what is your name?' I asked.

'Patience,' she answered.

'Patience? Ehen! You are my mother's namesake. That's her name,' I said, smiling.

'That's nice, o. So I am your mother's namesake,' she said, also smiling. She looked away from me at the sound of a motorcycle. It was a familiar sound. I turned around to look at who it was and saw that it was Papa.

'Your father has come. I am going inside,' she said and went inside. I waited for Papa at the door and greeted him when he came towards the door where I stood.

'*Miguo*, Papa,' I greeted.

'*Vrendo,*' he answered. 'You people have finished Catechism class?' he asked, like he did not know the class was already over.

'Yes, Papa,' I answered.

'Okay, that's good. Come inside and sit down. Where is Johwo?' he asked.

'She is inside,' I replied.

'*Oya, mo.* Your mother will be coming soon. I did not go to the house, I came straight to the church,' he informed.

'Okay, Papa.' We entered the church. Papa genuflected and dipped his right hand in the blue bowl containing holy water. It was placed on a tripod stand by the church door. He sprinkled some on his head, making the sign of the cross. I found Johwo sitting on the third pew of the middle row. I joined her. We knelt down to pray as we were taught to always do before Mass. Mama soon came. She sat with us. Papa led the Angelus after reading out the intentions for the Mass. Father Sixtus began Mass about ten minutes later. He apologised for the lateness as he had been to Warri and was just coming back. The church said his apology was accepted when he asked if they had accepted it like they had a choice of saying otherwise. We went home after the Mass. That evening Papa was in a good mood and he decided to tell us a story. He told us the story of how the stubborn Omena refused to heed her mother's words and had her beautiful face exchanged for that of a spirit. Papa began the story by clearing his throat first.

'In the village of Ole-era, spirits came roaming at a particular season. During that season, only male children and men were allowed to go out. Married women also went out before 2:00pm to get what they wanted from the market then made sure to be back in their homes before the spirits attacked them. The spirits exchanged their demonic faces with the beautiful faces of young maidens.' Papa paused to drink water. We waited keenly for him to continue. I saw the images of the ugly spirits cutting off their faces and exchanging it with the girls' faces. Papa continued.

'Omena being the only child of her widowed mother was treated like an egg, her mother took care of her and gave her all she wanted. She was a very beautiful girl. And the season of the spirits soon came that year. Parents started locking up their female children at home. That Friday morning, her mother decided to go to the market to buy ingredients to prepare *egusi* soup. She cooked yam for Omena and asked her to heat up the stew when she wanted to eat the food. There were only two matchsticks left in the box. Her mother told her that she should light one and boil the yam. If she ran out of matches, she should eat the cooked yam with red oil. Omena said yes to her mother's words like an obedient daughter. After her mother had left for the market, she cleaned the house and kept the dirt in a parker which she left behind the door to throw out when the spirits had gone. She settled down to heat up the stew but both matchsticks went off. She could not eat the stew cold and she had lost interest in the red oil. She decided to go and buy a matchbox outside. She said to herself, *'If Mama can go out, me too can.'* She opened the door and went out. It was quiet outside. She walked briskly. The shop where she wanted to buy the matchstick which was farther off her house became closer. She wondered within herself but said nothing and went in. She called to the seller and a voice replied that he was coming. Soon, the bearer of the voice came out and she realised it was a spirit. Before she could run out, the spirit jeered at her and took her face. She ran back to the house and fell on her bed in tears. She was even afraid to look in the mirror. She heard the door creek and open. Her mother had returned'

'*Gbam, gbam!*' Johwo said, trying to make the sound used when terrible things were about to happen in Nigerian movies.

Mama laughed. Papa continued.

'Her mother then called out to her. 'Omena, my eye. My daughter, where are you?'

Then her mother heard sorrowful singing and followed the voice to find a creature with a beastly face sitting behind the door.

'Who are you? Where is my child?' she asked, frightened.

'Mama, it is I. I am Omena. I disobeyed you and went out. Now, my mother, they have taken my face and left me to suffer with this one,' Omena answered, in tears. Her mother fell to the floor in tears and neighbours came to see what had happened,' Papa ended the story.

'Papa, is that the end?' I asked.

'Yes, Atarhe'

'What happened to Omena after that?' Johwo asked.

'Children, your Papa have said the story, so what are the lessons that you learnt?' Mama asked.

'That we should be obedient to our parents,' Johwo said.

'Yes, that is why the fifth commandment says what?' Papa asked.

'Honour your father and your mother so that your days on earth may be long,' Johwo and I answered.

Mama smiled. 'Okay, enough stories for one night. I am tired o. Let's pray and sleep', she said.

We grumbled in protest. We wanted to hear more stories but Mama walked us to the room after we prayed and said our good nights.

Mama went to the parlour from our room. She and Papa usually stayed up for a little while after we went to bed before they went to sleep. On Sunday, it was a visiting priest who said Mass. Father Sixtus had gone to one of the out-stations for Mass. The priest was also interesting to listen to, compared to Father Sixtus, he treated the homily very well that I did not find myself sleeping off as I usually did. We greeted the priest after Mass and went home. I awaited the test results with great anxiety. I wanted to see an improvement. I wanted scores that will get me going cartwheels. I would sing and dance and shout on top of my voice if I passed the test. Then, I would say a big thank you to Miss Mary-Rose.

The long awaited Monday morning came. I dressed smartly. Mama had bought me a new pair of socks. I had a haircut and was ready for school. When Miss Mary-Rose called the class monitor to hand him the notes to share out the owners, I found my heart in my mouth. I waited for my book drawing figures on my desk with my pencil. The book dropped on my table. I sat stiff. I shut my eyes as I turned the cover page open and flipped the leaves to the page where I had written the tests. I got that feeling, the one they called butterflies in my stomach when I saw the scores. It was a huge improvement for me, the type that I had never even thought of before. I saw Miss Mary-Rose smile at me from her table. I smiled back. Then, she winked. I smiled back again. She turned to the work on her table. I saw the scores 9,11,12,14,15,15 and 16 in Maths, English, Health Education, Elementary science, B/K and Urhobo respectively. And handwriting, I had 8. The class became rowdy as pupils exchanged notes and talked about their different scores. Chinyere had done very well and so did Dami.

'Dami, see I got 9 in Maths,' I said to him, happily.

He smiled. 'Atarhe, you improved. Thank God,' he said, looking at the notebook.

I did not have lessons with Miss Mary-Rose for that day but she was happy that I had made progress. She spoke to me before I left for home.

'My little girl,' she said, hugging me. She really squeezed me tight that I could not force myself out of her arms. 'I am so proud of you, Atarhe. Look how far you have come. You are making progress. You may not have passed the way you wanted to but you did beautifully. I am proud of you,' she said, releasing me from her embrace.

'Miguo, Aunty,' I greeted her in appreciation.

'Vrendo, my dear. Take this two hundred naira and buy biscuit, you hear?' She handed me a clean two hundred naira note.

I grinned. 'Thank you so much, Aunty'.

I went home to tell a happy expectant mother of the good news about my test results. She stood up, carried me on her back for a few seconds and danced in a funny way. She did same with Johwo. She was very happy to see our success. Mama had never thought that one day I would be this better. When I told her of the money Miss Mary-Rose had given me, she prayed for blessings upon her and her household.

'God bless this young lady and her family. She has been a blessing. May our Lady, mother of all bless her and grant her, her desires,' Mama prayed.

'Amen!' Johwo and I said.

Dear lettar,

It is all becoming bettar with each day that passes. I passed my test. I scored 9 in Maths without anybody adding mark for me. miss Mary-rose is just a very good aunty. I just like her very much and her uncle too. They have treating me and making me bettar. They are publishing my lettars and doing great things for me. lettar how can I thank them. God knows how to use peple o. This aunty is ~~God~~ God that is using her to help us. The 3rd term will soon finish now and then, I would know how well I improved. Even communion time will reach. This christmas that is coming we will recieve the sacrament. we will. By that time, Mama tummy will have been big like ball. I am very happy that we will na have a younger brother. Did I tell you that is Mudiaga that I will call him? Yes, that's the name that I will give him as his senior sistar. I am just happy.

Your friend,
Atarhe

I submitted six more letters to Miss Mary-Rose, making the number of letters for the compilation amount to forty. I any afterwards did not submit. I left them for myself.

10

It was already two weeks after the test and a week to the promotion examinations. Mama's belly was bulging out gradually. It was like the size of my sleeping wrapper rolled up in her dress at the stomach region. Johwo and I played, rubbing it. Mama would brush us off playfully asking us not to disturb her child because he or she is sleeping and waiting to come out to the world. I was waiting anxiously and gracefully for my brother to be born. I knew he was a boy. My instincts were so strong that it was a male. Mr Alfred had called for me to come over to his place to see the designs of the cover for the book. I went to his place with Miss Mary-Rose and we picked one out of four that he brought to us. The one we chose had this telling picture. There was a hand with a pencil writing on a sheet of paper the words 'Dear Lettar'. The background colour was sea green which gave this cool impression. I liked it. Before we left, he took out two thousand naira from the ottoman beside him and handed it over to me. I thanked him and we left. He had titled it *Lettars From an Imbecile- A diary of thoughts'*. He told me that I spelt letter in the wrong way but that was part of the style of the book.

With the exams fast approaching, I worked hard enough to pass. I also worked hard on my Catechism. Christmas was not far away. August was drawing nearer to the end of the term. I wanted to pass. I wanted to make Papa and Mama happy in the very best way I could. I had written on Monday morning before school.

Dear lettar,

Mama stomach have become very big. Me and Johwo use to play with it every time. She will tell us to leave her baby that is sleeping alone. We will laugh and keep on rubbing the stomach. Exam is coming now. I have passed test. Will I pass exam too? I know I will. Slowly, I have become a new girl. I know you are happy. Thank you for been there with me. i am glad to be your friend. And, we have seen the book cover and it is very fine. I like it. Lettar, this is very good. I am just feeling happy. then my name will be on the cover of a book. Do you know I have not be spelling you wrong since. He said it is letter but I like the way I write your name. The name of the book is even Lettars from an ~~imbecill~~ imbecile. I like the name. Parents who think that they cannot accept thier children because of one problem or the other will learn like Papa has learnt to always take care of their children because they can never ever tell when that child will become some great.

Your friend,
Atarhe

I studied exercises daily to help my improvement in the up-coming promotion exams. Mama had promised to get me and Johwo presents if we wrote well. I spent less time playing and watching TV and the rest of the time was spent studying. I was expecting the release of the book in seven months time. That would be in the month of February, the year after.

Miss Mary-Rose gave me series of homework every day to study and solve at home after school according to the exam time-table. With her around, everything was better and graceful. I did not know what more I wanted. What more I could ask for. God had made my world anew and placed everything I asked for on a platter of gold.

The week flew by and exams began. The exams were to last from Monday to Friday. With two subjects on the first and second day and single subjects the rest of the days. We wrote our exams and by Friday, the results were out and we went to receive our report cards. After we had collected them at Miss Mary-Rose's desk, we opened our cards to check for our results. I was stunned to 41/50 in the space for position. I looked further to see the average position of 53.8. I had done very well by passing the average mark even with just three marks. The remarks of Miss Mary-Rose were heartfelt ones. She wrote in her beautiful handwriting: **Atarhe is an obedient student, she has improved greatly and should keep on trying. Promoted to the next class.**

Gift had come second in class that term. Benson came first, Dami and one other boy, Joshua both came seventh.

Coming in the forty-first position in class and being ahead of nine persons was a huge achievement for me. The highest position that I have ever had before Miss Mary-Rose came to the school was the second to last place. Johwo had also done very well that term. She came second place from fifth place. The increase in my average was a great one for me because I had an average of 35.8 the last term. It was a whooping increase of eighteen marks. The holidays were going to be an enjoyable one for me. I may not travel to other countries like rich children in private schools did, I may not travel to other states or cities to spend the holidays with friends of family but just knowing that I have passed and have been promoted is enough for me to have a happy holiday.

Mama was very happy at our results. She was happy that I was promoted, happy that I did not fail. She prepared Jollof rice and fried pieces of beef and also bought bottles of soft drinks for us to felicitate with on that day. She danced in those funny steps of hers to our success. The holiday was just getting started and the air smelt of good things. We usually went to the shop with Mama. At times, Johwo and I stayed back at home. Mama started teaching me, and even Johwo, how to cook varieties of food such as boiled rice, *egusi* soup, stew, coconut rice and a few other simple meals.

We went to Mass daily. Once, Father Sixtus joked about me and Johwo coming to stay in the parish house with him. It was a joke but I had imagined us eating with the fancy breakable and ceramic plates and cups in the big-sized dining table. I imagined Father taking us in his Hyundai jeep to the town and places of interest which children enjoyed. I imagined him telling us to go to bed and to pray before we sleep. I also spent the holidays by reading. I read in view of the next session. I did not want a short-lived success.

Dami came visiting one Saturday afternoon. He had asked for directions to my place. Papa was not at home while Mama was in the shop with Johwo. When he came, we sat outside on the brown bench in veranda.

'Dami, how are you?' I asked him.

'I am very fine. I said lemme come and see you today.' He said.

'I did not know that you know where my house is. Who showed you the place?' I asked

'I asked Johwo before vacation day that she should describe your house for me.' he answered.

'Ehen, investigator. Let us go to my Mama's shop. Johwo is there with her too,' I said to him.

'Okay. Let us go'

'Wait for me, I want to lock the house first,' I said to him. I went inside, picked the house key from inside the brown sprayed wooden cup carved in the shape of a wine glass where the keys were kept. I made sure to close all doors and locked the front door with the silver coloured security padlock. I locked the front door and we went to the shop. Mama welcomed him warmly after he greeted her with the usual, *Miguo*.

'Vrendo, my dear,' she said, in reply to his greeting. 'How are your parents?'

'They are fine, Ma,' he answered.

'Thank God. You are welcome. Pick biscuit and eat, my son,' she said to him.

Dami looked at me. I did not say anything to him. I could see it in his eyes that he didn't. He want to take any. He finally spoke up to Mama's hearing.

'No, thank you, Ma,' he said to her.

Mama looked at me and giggled, then she said to me, 'Tarhe, you did not tell your friend that he cannot come here and leave without eating?' she turned to Dami, 'Pick two biscuits and even if you don't want to eat it here, you will take it home.'

'Okay, Ma. *Miguo,*' he greeted, showing appreciation. He picked two biscuits: one *Noreos* and the other, *Shapes* biscuit. He opened the Noreos and started eating it. He stayed long enough for Mama to finish making Johwo's hair with the local rubber thread. Johwo and I saw him off to the junction of our street where he walked on by himself to his place.

'This your Dami friend is a good friend,' Johwo said.

'Yes. Let us go back to the shop. Mama will be waiting for us already,' I said.

We went back to the shop and helped Mama with the sales. Like I said, people would start calling Mama, *Babuwa.* I was right. Most people who came to her shop to buy things called her *Babuwa.* Before bed that night, I wrote,

Dear lettar,

Dami came visiting today. I took him to see Mama. I was happy to have taken him to Mama. Mama even treated him well too. She gave him biscuits. He was now forming that he did not want to eat but Mama say that he must eat. I was laughing at him in my mind. I am even smiling now as I yam talking to you. Dami was different today. He did not look like the way he use to dress in school. He was wearing one jeans trouser and one blue shirt. He was fine. Dami is a good boy. Johwo even said it too. I want, Mudiaga, my small brother to be like him. Mama say she is going to born him in November. I want them to born him on the 15th. I just like that day. We will na do thanks giving in Mass and dedication and they will baptise him the way Father have been baptising other children. Hmmmmmmmmm, I cannot wait so that that day will reach quick. Lettar, by Febuary, the book will have come outside. I hope that it is a good book and that it will sell well. I want to sleep.

Your friend,
Atarhe

Most of the parishioners in the church had been told already of my success in school and the up-coming publishing of the book. I had thought Mama had spearheaded the broadcast of the news but adding to my list of surprises, it was Papa who had been spreading the news out like a newly employed DRTV correspondent. Even other children started relating more with me and I was no longer the shy girl who never speaks to anybody. The women of CWO were not left out in the jubilation with Mama.

143

'Yes, o, my God has favoured me amongst my fellow women,' Mama said to them, after Mass on Friday evening. She said it in almost the same tone as the Blessed Virgin Mary would have used in saying the Magnificant when she visited Elizabeth. Most times, the women did a funny dance like the type Mama did when she was happy. They moved one of their legs forward, throwing out their arms and then rolled their waists without any rhythm. They would then hug Mama at the end of the dance. At other times, they did what was called the CWO clap, hitting their hands to create a *Kpam-kpam* sound and singing the words. 'Jesus, I love you, Amen!' after each *kpam-kpam* clap. Papa even told me that for the first time, he was proud of me.

As the first term drew closer, I was both happy and sad. I was happy at my promotion. Happy at my success. Happy that I did not fail. But I was sad also. Sad because I would have a new class teacher. A new teacher that was not going to be like Miss Mary-Rose. No one could be like her. My fear only subdued when on one of her visits, she assured me of teaching me as usual in the evenings and that she was always going to check up on me and care for me as she had always done. She had come visiting a number of times during the holidays. On one of such visits, Mama compelled her to eat starch and *owho* with her. I never ate starch. I could not swallow it and it was too sticky like evostick gum for me to chew it like I chewed eba. Moreover, Mama used it to wash clothes to make them hard and I wondered how one thing can be used for food and for washing clothes at the same time. Mama had explained several times that as washing clothes, the use was different and as a meal it was also different. Her explanations never for a moment changed my rotion. Miss Mary-Rose had become a member of my family and I was happy to be a pupil of hers. August ran out soon and September ushered itself in. The August break contrasted greatly with the seven days rain that fell in July. The dry air could almost be compared to the harmattan season. School was soon to be in session. Mama bought us new notebooks, pencils, erasers, sharpeners, biros. I was very happy to have my own biro. I had graduated from the use of pencils to the use of blue-inked biros. I spent the week before the resumption writing my letters with one of the biros. They were Leo smart and bic biros. I was excited to tell my letter about it.

Dear lettar,

Guest what? I have started using biro to write. Mama bought four of them for me. I am writing with the first one now. But I am not too happy. she, I am talking about Miss Mary-rose, she will not be my class teachar again. it is paining me that a new teachar will now teach me. I will miss her very much. But, the day she came, I told you that she said that she will not abandon me but will still be teaching me in the evuning like before. She is a good woman. mama's CWO friend's in church have been happy and celebrating since because I pass my exams. mama did not have to beg teachars to promote me. lettar, this year is the best year of my life that I have been alife.

Your friend,
Atarhe

145

The new session began. The first day seemed different but interesting. Possibly different because Miss Mary-Rose was not there in my class. I had greeted her that morning before going to my class. She asked me to come to her class by break. We were asked to seat in threes as usual with a boy in our middle. Dami and Chinyere remained my seat partners. It was good having them as my seatmates again. We chatted away about events that happened during the holidays. I told them about the rejoicing that took place among Mama and her friends and even with Papa.

'What do you expect, Tarhe?' Chinyere asked, when I told her how happy Mama was. 'She is just happy that her daughter is finally progressing,' she added.

'Yes, we are just happy for you. Many people were just happy that you passed,' Dami said.

'I'm not sure those ones have anything good in their mouth to say,' Chinyere was referring to Gift and Beatrice who were walking towards our desk.

'Atarhe, hello,' Gift said, when they got to the desk.

I did not find the words in my mouth to reply her greeting.

'We just wanted to say we are sorry for the way we were treating you,' Beatrice said.

'Okay. I was not angry with you people,' I told them.

'Thank you,' they both said.

They also said hi and rendered apologies to Dami and Chinyere before they went back to their seats.

'They have luck that they said sorry,' Dami said.

'Yes o. They have tire to quarrel,' I said.

'Just leave them,' Chinyere said to me. We continued our chit-chat before Mrs Orogun, our stout class teacher, asked us to introduce ourselves one after the other so that she could know us better.

'I know you, Atarhe. The miracle girl. How are your parents?' she asked, when I stood up to introduce myself.

'They are fine, Ma,' I said.

I went to see Miss Mary-Rose during break. She asked me a number of questions. The questions were a bit too much that I felt she was suffocating me with them. She just wanted to make sure I was feeling alright in my new class, even just on the first day. She had told me she had grown so fond of me that she feels like crying knowing that I was no longer in her class.

At first, I could not cope along well with the class, perhaps, because my favourite teacher was not there with me. There were two newly admitted pupils in the class- a boy and a girl. There were also two others who repeated. Most of the students were getting on with the new class, others were adjusting while some others like myself adjusted to the new life soon enough.

That afternoon when we got home, Mama had gone to the clinic for her ante-natal, Johwo dropped her school bag on the chair. I picked it and went to the room. We soaked *garri* and ate it with the groundnut Johwo had gone out to buy. Papa's school had also resumed work that day. It was just the two of us at home.

'Johwo,' I called. She was sitting next to me. There was no power supply.

'Yes'

'Do you think that now that Aunty Mary-Rose have left my class that I will still be doing well?,' I asked.

'Yes, *na*. Aunty Mary-Rose have even say that she will be helping you. You would do well like before,' She said, with such assurance in her words.

'Okay, Johwo,' I said.

'Are you afraid?' Johwo asked.

I nodded.

'Atarhe, don't be *o*. You know that you are even going to have a book. My sister will now be an author. I will now be an author's sister,' she said, smiling at me.

I smiled back at her. She looked different. Maybe because we were getting along better than before. She had a new sisterly look, a better one. The one I always wanted her to give me.

'Do you want to play cards? This one that NEPA don't want to bring light. Let me go and bring them,' she said, getting up from the carpeted floor which we sat on.

'Okay. I will win you,' I said.

'You go old die,' she said, in pidgin.

'Ehen, oya come back,' I said, as she walked through the narrow passage to our room.

'Let me bring them, *jare*,' she answered back.

She went to our room to get the playing cards and we played. She won me thrice in a row repeating the winning words 'Check up' with so much gracefulness each time. I laughed. She laughed also. I was happy. She was happy.

Mama came back. She bought guavas. I loved eating guavas. Johwo loved them too. They had this taste that agreed wonderfully with my tongue. I ate most of them. Mama always warned to spit out the seeds saying that it caused one to develop appendicitis. I always spat out the seeds heeding to Mama's advice. Johwo chewed every bit of it from skin to flesh to seeds. I wished we had a guava tree- one that I would pluck fruits from and sit under with the cool breeze blowing over my face. We ate the guavas.

Miss Mary-Rose called Papa on the phone that evening.

'Hello, Mary-Rose. How are you?' Papa said, answering the call. He paused to listen to her response.

'This one that you are calling, hope no problem?' He paused again.

'Ehen, by Monday? Is it okay for Atarhe to miss school?' he asked. I wondered what they were talking about.

'Papa Atarhe, *oyin die,*' Mama asked, wanting to be fed on the topic of the call. Papa was still on the phone.

'I am coming,' he replied, in Urhobo. He continued, 'Ehen? Okay. Thank you.' he hung up. He dropped the phone on the coffee table and sat down on the chair.

'Atarhe's teacher said that they want to interview her on Monday,' he said.

'The book people?' Mama asked.

'Yes.'

'But Atarhe cannot miss school on a Monday,' Mama said.

'That's what I said myself,' Papa said. 'So, I told her to tell Mr Avwenaughe that they should try and fix it on Friday,' he added.

'Okay, that's better.'

'Papa, is it like all those TV interview,' I asked.

'I don't know but just prepare, you hear?'

'Okay, Papa.'

Dear lettar,

Guest what? Bettar news have come. They say that they want to interview me. But I am afraid. I don't know how to talk in public places. I yam afraid of plenty people in one place. My English is not even good. What do I do? Tell me. I don't know. But it is a good thing sha. I will talk to big people. I will talk to writers and they will show me on tv. Lettar, they will show your Atarhe on telivision. Mama is happy. even Papa. I will dream this night. I 1know that I will dream plenty plenty. I will dream of talking to those big men. What will I wear? I will tell Mama to buy me a fine dress. Good night. Johwo is already sleeping. Let me go and sleep. See you tomorow.

Your friend,
Atarhe.

I rolled over my bed that night gathering the sheets away from Johwo. I dreamed. I dreamed that I was in a large office with renowned writers and they all applauded for me. I kept smiling all through. I dreamed another dream. It was also beautiful but I could not remember it. I woke up after the dream. The time was 4:00am. I slept back.

11

Mr Avwenaughe had met with the firm and the interview was fixed on Friday. I had been practicing on my speech with Johwo as my trainer. Mama had said she would buy me a new dress. By Tuesday, she had told me that we would both go to the market to shop for something presentable. But she was surprised and glad when I returned home from school with a nylon bag in which there was a smart matching shirt and skirt. Mrs Avwenaughe, Mr Alfred's wife had bought them for me. Mama called Miss Mary-Rose asking her to extend her greetings to the family especially to her aunty who did well by buying me the clothes. I was grateful to them, not only were the clothes beautiful but they were expensive. Mama could have never bought those. Moreover, it saved Mama of the expenses. I tried them on. They fitted perfectly.

'*Omote oyibo me,*' Mama praised me. 'She just knows your size. See as you are looking fine.' She smiled as she spoke.

'Mama, she is just fine. Mama, I will buy this type too,' Johwo said.

'Okay, Johwo. Let's wait and see,' Mama said.

'Atarhe,' Johwo said, turning to me. 'We will be wearing the dress together,' she said.

I laughed. I knew it was a joke. We never wore the same size of anything- from shoes to clothes. I was taller than her and she was fatter than I was. Johwo said we should go and practice more on speech after I had changed from the clothes. She played the role of the interviewer asking me questions while I answered.

'Welcome to this interview, Miss Atarhe Onanefe. How are you?' she said. She held a biro as her microphone. I wondered if in the interview there would be microphones. I had never talked in one before.

'I yam....'

'Not yam that we eat,' she said. 'Am,' she corrected.

'Okay. I am fine, sir,' I said, taking the correction.

'So, how are you feeling concerning the book release?' she asked, pronouncing concern as consign.

'I am happy that they want to release the book in colla....' I stopped. 'What is that word that you said that time again?' I asked her.

'Collaboration,' she said.

'Ehen. Collaboration.'

'Let me ask you again.' She asked the same question again.

'I am happy that the book in collaboration with Mr Alfred is going to be out for people to read,' I said, saying collaboration very slowly in other not to make a mistake in the pronunciation or bite my tongue in the process. We practiced further. We laughed. We played. Then, we weared out ourselves. We went inside. Just as we entered the parlour, power came on. Johwo ran to put on the television switch. I was staring at the TV with such keenness that one would say I was enjoying the programme. But, I was far away. I was far from the TV, far from the walls of the house. I was in a world of my own, dreaming about the interview, dreaming about what would happen after the interview. What would happen after the book was released.

Dear lettar,
Uncle Afred's wife bought for me a new dress. It is a skirt and a shirt. Ash colour. She said I should wear it to the interview. Johwo have been giving me speech practice. Even aunty Mary-rose have been teaching me. she is going to follow me to the interview. She will take excuse in school. I will wear my fine dress and I would now go to warri. I will be on TV. Mama will watch me that is if there is light. I am waiting for the day to come. I would talk well. I will talk with the English that Johwo have been teaching me. I will. present my self, the way aunty Mary-rose tought me to do. I will make you proud. I will tell you everything.

Your friend,
Atarhe.

The interview was scheduled for noon on Friday. I was to arrive at the publishing house by 11.00am. I went to school that morning. Miss Mary-Rose and myself were to leave for Warri at about 10.00am. She had taken excuse for me and herself in school. I had two subjects before she came to my class. We boarded an *okada* to the Avwenaughe's house. Mr Alfred was already in Warri. Miss Mary-Rose took me to her room for me to dress up. I wore the shirt and skirt Mrs Avwenaughe had bought for me. Mrs Avwenaughe came into the room and also helped in dressing me up. I had my hair brushed. Miss Mary-Rose gave me her necklace and earring to put on. I put some perfume on my body. It smelt nice and expensive. When all was ready, we got into the car and Mrs Avwenaughe took us to the car park where we left for Warri. We arrived at the press. Mr Alfred had one of the assistants take me and Miss Mary-Rose round the library. We looked at the books on the shelf as we walked from shelf to shelf without opening even one of them. By fifteen minutes to 12:00pm, Miss Mary-Rose asked me to sit down in the dressing room. She applied some perfumed powder on my face, then she brought out a baby pink-coloured lip gloss and was about to apply it on my lips.

'Aunty, Mama don't use to give us wet lip,' I said.

'Don't worry. It's just a little so that your lip will not be dry,' she said.

She applied some on my lips and asked me to move them over each other to let them blend doing so herself as a demo. I did as she said. It felt awkward to have lip gloss on my lips. It looked good though but different. Mr Alfred came and ushered me into the interview room. The room was air-condition tight. It was red carpeted and had book shelves in it. There was a long couch and two single armchairs. Mr Alfred and I sat on the sofa while the interviewers - a man and woman, sat on the single chairs. There was an audience made of a countable number of people, possibly forty persons. I was frightened by their number and their faces. I looked at my laps most times and the ceiling other times.

'Good day, Miss Atarhe, the new eye of Reality Press and Mr Alfred, the renowned Editor of Reality books. How are you today?' the man spoke.

'We are fine. Thank you,' Mr Alfred said.

'I am Simon Adeniji and with me here is the lovely, Anita Peters, bestselling author of *Lies in My Era,*' he introduced himself and the female. She must have been popular to receive such a title, bestselling. I did not exactly know what it meant.

'Nice to have you here today on this pre-publishing interview,' Anita Peters said, smiling. She was beautiful. Like Miss Mary-Rose. Miss Mary-Rose was in the audience.

'Thank you,' Mr Alfred said.

They started off by asking Mr Alfred some questions on the book and the audience got an opportunity to talk on it. I just laughed and giggled at points when I thought it was necessary to.

'Now, little star of the press,' Simon said to me. I smiled but it did not brighten my face. 'Tell us how you feel about this whole event?'

I could not find the words in my mouth. I looked at Mr Alfred, he gave me a nod to go ahead but the words were stuck in my throat. I found it hard to speak.

'I...I, hmmm. I'. I stopped. The audience were quiet.

'Maybe she is shy,' Anita said. 'Sweetheart, we are waiting,' she said, like a reminder that much was expected of me.

Miss Mary-Rose stood up in the audience. 'We should applaud the little girl first before we listen to her,' she suggested.

'Good lady,' Mr Alfred said.

The audience gave a loud applause for me. I looked at Miss Mary-Rose and smiled.

'Very well, the little reality writer must be ready to tell us how she feels,' Simon said.

'I am very happy that I have a book that would be publish...published for people to read and enjoy,' I said.

'That's a beautiful one,' Simon said.

'She sure is a wonderful child,' Anita added.

There were so many other questions thrown to both of us from Simon and Anita and the audience. They asked Mr Alfred how well I could cope with the book industry with my well known medical challenge. His answer made the subtle skin around my lips crinkle up into a smile.

'Atarhe has been called an imbecile, a child without a future but before our very own eyes she has created her own future. She has started it and she would finish glamorously,' he answered. The audience applauded. The interview came to an end at exactly 1:00pm. It was a one-hour programme. I ran to meet Miss Mary-Rose and she gave me a warm embrace. It felt good. It felt wonderful. Everything, the hug, the interview and me. We went out to eat at one of the famous eateries with Simon and Anita.

By 4:00pm that evening, Mr Alfred and Miss Mary-Rose dropped me off at home. The resounding *pim pim pim* of the car horn must have made Mama come out in a rush. Her wrapper loosely tied and she moved quickly with her protruding stomach almost like it was separately in front of her and she was behind it.

'Welicome, my people,' she said, saying welcome as welicome probably because she was happy. 'Good evening, sir,' she greeted Mr Alfred.

'Good evening, Madam,' he replied.

Mama asked me to go inside and eat. I told her I had eaten before coming. She insisted I go in and rest. Miss Mary-Rose said her goodbyes. They told Mama that they were in a hurry to get home. Moreso, they could not stay for any refreshments but Mama said the next time they come to her house, she would not accommodate such excuscs.

'My daughter, how was the interview?' Mama asked me after I had my evening bath. I and Mama did not go to evening mass, but Papa and Johwo did.

'Mama, it was very interesting. They say they would send us a copy of the video. I was afraid at first but later when people started to clap for me, I was happy.'

'Ehen!' Mama exclaimed, amused.

'Yes o. Even Uncle Alfred said that I am a good girl that would make it well in life,' I said.

'That is true, my daughter,' Mama said, 'You are my Oke,' she said.

I lay down on the couch and placed my head on her laps. I closed my eyes. I must have fallen asleep. I only woke up to see Papa and Mama with Johwo eating.

'*Miguo*, Papa,' I greeted him, yawning.

'Ehen, my dear. *Vrendo*,' he replied. 'Have you eaten?'

'Yes, Papa.'

'Okay. Your Mother has told me and your sister about the interview. You should go and sleep. *Dooh*,' he said.

'Okay, Papa. Good night, Papa. Good night, Mama. Good night, Johwo.' I went to the room and slept. I was tired. I did not dream that night. I slept and I woke up the next morning, Saturday.

Dear lettar,

Good morning. Yesterday I was very tired. The interview was very good. At first, I was afraid to talk but aunty Mary-rose said that they should clap for me and I felt bettar. I started to answer all the questions. Mr Alfred even said that I am a good girl with a great future. I have become known in school as the wonder girl. God has made things bettar for me and for papa and mama and Johwo.

Your friend,
Atarhe.

November. Two months after the interview. Mama was due. She would put to bed anytime soon. I had told her the name I wanted for my baby brother. She said she liked it. On a Monday evening, the 15th of November, when I got

158

back from school, Johwo who had gone ahead before me as I had evening lessons informed me that Mama had gone to the General hospital. She said Mama had called her sister, our Aunty Regina to come and accompany her to the hospital and she would call him when she got to the hospital. I prayed for her safe delivery. I went under her pillow to check if she forgot to take the Our Lady of Perpetual Help prayer leaflet with her. She had taken it. Johwo and I sat down and waited for them to come. Around seven in the evening, Papa came home. He informed us that Mama had been delivered of a baby boy. We jumped up, dancing and shouting in happiness.

'Johwo, did I not tell you that Mama will born boy?' I asked.

'Is true o,' she said. 'Papa, when will Mama come home?' she asked Papa.

'Don't worry, Mama will come tomorrow evening by God's grace,' Papa said.

'Okay. Thank God,' I said.

'Her sister is there, your Aunty Regina. She will be fine. Have you children eaten?' he asked.

'Yes, Papa. We ate *eba*,' I answered.

'Okay that's good. Let me go and eat. You people should sleep. There is morning Mass and school tomorrow,' he said, going to his room.

'Good night, Papa,' we said.

'*Etode,*' Papa said. We went to our room and Johwo and I talked about Mama's delivery and what our little brother looked like.

'Atarhe, what do you think he looks like?' she asked, as we both faced each other lying on the bed.

'He will be fine. Like Mama or like you,' I answered.

She smiled. 'I can't wait to carry him,' she said.

'Yes o. You are na a senior sister like me,' I said.

'Yes. We will tell Father Sixtus tomorrow after Mass. We will do baptism. I will tell my friends in school,' she said, excited.

'Yes. Let's sleep'

'Will you not tell your letter about Mudiaga?' she asked.

'I will tell him,' I said. I personalized my letter to be human, a trusted friend.

'I want to sleep. Go and tell him now so that we will sleep the same time,' she said.

'Okay.'

I went to the table. I wanted to tear out a page from my note but she offered me a page from her own note and asked that I say hi to the letter for her.

Dear lettar,

I bring you good news. My mama have born a baby boy. The one Papa have been waiting for. The one I named Mudiaga. Mama will come with him tomorrow. Everything is just becoming happy and graceful. I am just thanking God that he is doing everything well for us. Johwo said I should greet you. lettar, I am beginning to find myself without being afraid. One day, I would stop writing to you but I would never forget how much you helped me. I am just happy that you have given me the chance to use you to find myself. I know God made

160

write to you. I know he made me to start writing to you. god does wonder full things. I would love brother and sherish him and take care of him. I am tired already. Good night, dear friend.

Your friend,
Atarhe.

I went to bed, told Johwo good night and shut my eyes. I dreamed of my baby brother. I dreamed of carrying him strapped on my back and playing in the house.

Papa woke us up at around 4:30am to prepare for Mass. He gave us two hundred naira to buy food in school as Mama was not around to prepare food for us. We arrived at the church just in time for adoration to the blessed sacrament. At the end of Mass, we went to see Father Sixtus and we told him of the good news.

'Madam has given birth? God is good,' Father Sixtus said.

'Yes o. He is always good,' Papa said.

'Girls, how are you feeling?' he asked us.

'Very, very happy fada,' we said.

One of the church wardens in the church, a friend to Mama came to Father and asked Papa why Mama had not come to church. Papa told her of Mama's delivery and she praised God. The news did spread to other women that morning and they came greeting Papa before we left for school. More people sent the news out that Catechist Josefu's wife had given birth. I told Dami about Mama and the new baby.

'What does he look like?' he asked.

'I know he is fine but we have not seen him. My Mama is coming this evening. We will see him at last,' I told him. Miss Mary-Rose was very happy and said she would come to see Mama and the baby.

That evening, Mama came home in one of the parishioner's car. Papa said the lady had come to visit and just ceased the opportunity to bring Mama and the baby home. People from the church and from family and friends started visiting baby every day. We, Johwo and I, ran from school every day to meet baby. Johwo spent more time with him while I sometimes stayed back and had lessons. On Friday, Miss Mary-Rose came with me to see the five days old baby boy. I did not know she had bought a gift for Mudiaga until she brought out three packs of pampers napkin from the nylon bag she carried. She also gave Mama five thousand naira from Mr Alfred and his wife and another one thousand naira from herself. We thanked her and Mama and Papa asked her to extend their appreciation to the Avwenaughe family.

Our home smelt of baby powder. Pampers, cloth napkins, baby food and baby feeders were all over the place. Mudiaga only cried when he was hungry or tired or in pain or maybe sick. He never cried when someone carried him, even strange faces never made him cry. He loved being carried and Mama was happy to have him. So were we. Mama and Papa soon arranged for little Mudiaga's baptism. He was baptised with the name John Bosco. We never answered our baptismal names in my home. I was baptised Josephine, after Papa and Johwo was baptised Scholastical.

The way time flies baffles one. November, my brother was born and he was baptised. That same month, I had my third catechism test and I and Johwo passed. Now, it was December, the time of Christmas when everyone was happy and joyous. Christmas songs reigned supreme in the air and the Nine lessons and Carol took place. Dami's birthday came and I bought him a gift, funny though, it was a notebook and biro. He liked it. The church's Nine Lessons and Carol were scheduled for the 22nd of December. We attended. That was Mudiaga's first Christmas. And two days from then was my big day. It was a big day for Johwo too and for Papa and Mama. We were receiving our first holy communion, the sacrament of the Holy Eucharist. It was to take place during the vigil Mass. I asked Miss Mary-Rose to come and she did. Christmas vigil started at eight and finished by midnight. There were also candidates amongst us for baptism. They were baptised after the homily and the whole church renewed their baptismal vows. There were two old men from the Anglican Communion who converted to the Catholic faith. They took their vows, said the Apostle creed and were not baptised again. Papa had said that people from the Anglican church were not asked to re-baptise because their baptism was accepted in the Catholic church.

During the time for communion, we had our candles lit. And we went forward and knelt by the altar and received the body and blood of our Lord. Mama felt fulfilled. I felt more than fulfilled, if there was something like that. Things had turned happily for me and family. This Christmas was the happiest of all. Johwo and I went to the Parish house with Mama and Mudiaga on Christmas day. I wrote my letter all about it. That was the last letter I addressed with the words, 'Dear lettar.'

12

The happy beginning, not ending.

The fulfilment one always wants comes with the things you put your whole heart, mind and soul on. I put my heart on being a better child, on being like a normal child despite my obvious abnormalities. I was now officially Atarhe Onanefe, co-author of *Lettars From An Imbecile- A diary of thoughts.* I was no longer the scared little girl with no future. The first book I ever wrote was selling well in the book market. The beginning of a career that I wanted, that I loved. I had found my first love in writing. The copies of the book were all over town and going wider around the country and soon enough other countries in the African continent.

Better things happened with time. Mr Alfred surprised my family when he said he was sending me on a scholarship to one of the special boarding schools in England. I was shocked. I don't know if that is the word to use but I was shocked. I did not expect that would come. Mama and Papa were very grateful and so was I. I would come home only during the long holidays and would stay with his sister during the mid-term breaks.

I was going to miss a lot of people: my baby brother, my parents, my sister, Miss Mary-Rose, Mr Alfred, Father Sixtus, the church and Dami. Johwo once asked me if I liked Dami. I knew what she meant and I answered her that Dami was a brother to me. Although, there were times, I felt I wanted more with him but what do we know? We are just children. As Papa always say, you children have a beautiful life ahead. Dami was my guardian angel and best friend. I would miss him like my other self. I wrote the last letter that I ever wrote for my collection. But this time, it was to God.

Dear God,

This one is for you. You have made me better. And you have brought people to help me. I am just happy to have been favoured by you. Ten years of my life was not normal but you had a big surprise for me. This is the best thing that ever happened to me. I have found myself in you. you have made whole. I made new friends and met good people. Protect this people for me. Bless them and provide for them. I am going far away from home. To a new place. Take me there and protect my family. I will say good bye to friends and family but I would come back to them, a better child and write more books and be a good child. You have made know so much that things that you do not expect come to you. Indeed you are right about everything and everything is a blessing. Extend these blessings to good people. Take care of my family, Papa and Mama, Miss Mary-Rose, Dami, Chinyere, Johwo, my baby brother Mudiaga. Bless the good people who help me. I love you. Amen.

Your daughter,
Atarhe.

I have come to the end of my story but not the end of my life. This life of mine is just beginning. I had hoped, I had faith, I had patience. That is all that ever mattered and will always matter. Now, I have a future to face. I wonder what the life ahead holds for me.

THE END

Printed in the United States
By Bookmasters